CHRISTMAS AT THE ROCKIN' K

HELLUVA ENGINEER, BOOK 2

SHIRLEY PENICK

CHRISTMAS AT THE ROCKIN' K

Copyright 2021 by Shirley Penick

All rights reserved. No part of this work may be reproduced in any fashion without the express written consent of the copyright holder

CHRISTMAS AT THE ROCKIN' K is a work of fiction. All characters and events portrayed herein are fictitious and are not based on any real persons living or dead.

Photography by JW Photography

Cover Models: Cyle Wood and Rachel Croon

Contact me:

www.shirleypenick.com

www.facebook.com/ShirleyPenickAuthor

To sign up for Shirley's Monthly Newsletter, sign up on my website or send email to shirleypenick@outlook.com, subject newsletter.

CHAPTER 1

*B*renda Stratton put the last piece of luggage in the back of her Range Rover. Her roommate Tracy locked the door to their rented duplex, and carried a small cooler which she put in the backseat, along with the Christmas gifts they planned to exchange in a week.

"It's only a two-hour drive," Brenda said laughing.

Her roommate was as tiny as Brenda was herself, but she ate a whole lot more. The only thing the two of them had in common was their height. Tracy was dark-haired with the lightest blue eyes Brenda had ever seen, they were nearly clear, she had a nose ring and three earrings in each ear. She had a curvy body that drew every man's attention.

Brenda, on the other hand, had blonde hair with violet eyes and a slender shape, with a lot less curves. Darn it. She had one set of earring holes and nothing else pierced or tattooed. She dressed conservatively while Tracy pushed the fashion envelope, always trying the newest trend.

"I know, but I get hungry after classes, it will probably be three hours or more before we eat. Besides the fruit won't last three weeks, so we might as well eat it. And we'll get thirsty."

"And the cookies?"

Tracy shrugged. "We can keep them in our room for snack emergencies. We don't know when or what they eat on the ranch."

Brenda had to agree with that one. "Since it's a cattle ranch I assume there won't be a beef shortage, but who knows about anything else."

The girls got into the Range Rover and buckled up. They drove about a half mile and stopped at a lovely, three-story, Victorian house, where their mentors lived. Brenda was a grad student assistant to Professor Steve Sampson and Tracy was the same to his wife, Dr. Patricia Decatur-Sampson. The couple had been married only a few months, but they already had a baby on the way.

Their mentors met them in the driveway. Steve said, "The Rav4 is packed with all the geology and mine reclamation test equipment, and every other possible thing we might need for our time in the mountains. We just need to stow our luggage in your car Brenda, then we can be on our way."

"Great, I have the destination programmed in my GPS, but I plan to follow you."

"Good. I've got the Rockin' K programmed in too. Let's move out. The less driving in the dark we have to do, the better."

Patricia walked up. "It will still be mostly dark driving, this time of year."

"Then, let's get going. Spirit Lake here we come."

As they got moving Brenda said, "We've never gone west on I-70. Any time we've gone to Rocky Mountain National Park we've started in Estes Park, so we've always driven I-70 eastbound."

"Should be fun. Provided it's not snowy."

"I have chains, just in case."

Tracy said, "Chains and all kinds of emergency winter gear. You spent a fortune in that store."

"I can afford it." Brenda shrugged, she had more money than she could ever spend from her trust fund, and she was going into a high-paying career. "I'd rather have too much winter gear than need something and freeze to death. Besides that, I might need it when I'm a real engineer next year."

"I don't want to talk about you leaving me. We still haven't been to all the National Parks."

Both the girls had been to Rocky Mountain National Park. It was the closest national park to the school. They'd made a vow to see every single national park in the country. They had a big wall map in their duplex that had all the national parks on it. And they put up a red star next to each one, after they had visited them.

"You'll be finished in a year. Besides maybe I'll go to work for a company based in Colorado."

"With five hundred thousand mines needing reclamation, Colorado and the surrounding area are just a drop in the bucket. I wouldn't be at all surprised if that company that Steve used to work for in Virginia didn't snap you right up. You are Steve's mentee after all."

"Yeah, but he hasn't been back on campus for a whole year, yet. It's not like he's had significant input into my education. Besides I can work wherever I choose, I'm not in a huge rush to have to pick whichever company comes calling first."

Tracy sighed. "Lucky you."

Brenda glanced at her friend; she knew Tracy didn't make friends easily. Numerous foster homes did not lend to long time friendships. And she didn't have a trust fund to fall back on, she would need to find a job immediately after leaving school. "Don't worry. I'll badger whoever I do go to work for that they need a brilliant geologist on their staff."

Her friend laughed. "Sounds good."

Fortunately, the roads were clear… ish, at least as clear as they got in the winter in Colorado, at that elevation. The road crews had been out, and the highway had been plowed and sanded, so they didn't have any trouble.

When they got through the Eisenhour tunnel and were on the other side of the continental divide both girls let out a breath that they had been holding.

Tracy said, "We made it."

"We did, the roads really are well maintained."

"The weather app said to expect harsher weather later in the week. I still kind of thought when we came out of the tunnel, we would hit a blizzard, but the skies are clear over here, too."

Brenda glanced at the outside temperature display. "It's cold enough."

"Yeah, clear skies don't hold in the heat like clouds do. Plus, we're three-thousand feet higher in elevation than we were."

"Good thing we both have nice warm coats."

Tracy laughed. "And a nice warm car heater."

"Even better."

When they got to the town of Spirit Lake, Brenda turned on the GPS, even though she was following Steve. She wanted to know the route to the ranch from town. It was a quick trip. They'd made good time, so it was not quite seven when they arrived.

Brenda said, "I hope it isn't too late for dinner. Don't ranchers and farmers, and people like that normally eat early?"

Tracy shrugged. "They are probably deliberately holding dinner for us."

When they turned off the main road onto a dirt one and drove under a sign that read Rockin' K, Brenda knew they were at the right place. There was a cattle guard that they drove over, apparently to keep the cows in.

Tracy said in almost a whisper, "Do you think we'll see any cows or cowboy activity?"

"I have no idea."

They went down the long driveway until a large house, and a large barn came into view. There was an enormous trailer attached to a huge truck. They were offloading horses which answered the cowboy question.

Tracy goggled. "I guess we will."

All the men had on jeans, boots, hats, gloves, and heavy denim jackets. Many of the hats were baseball caps, which totally blew Brenda's image of the American cowboy. Only a couple of them had on actual cowboy hats.

One of the men stepped aside and walked toward Steve's window. Brenda couldn't help but notice the man filled out his jeans exquisitely. She watched him talk to Steve and he pointed toward the side of the barn. Steve nodded and drove Patricia's Rav4 toward where the man had pointed. Brenda managed to follow Steve, but she'd had to tear her eyes away from the cowboy.

He was very attractive, she guessed he was a little bit older than she was. But a darn good-looking man. Brenda parked her Range Rover and both she and Tracy got out of the car and stretched after the long drive. She noticed several pairs of eyes watching their movements and nearly blushed. Until she thought about the fact she was going to a college where girls were a definite minority, she couldn't figure out how this situation differed from school, but somehow it just did.

Several other men had joined the first guy. The four engineers met at the back of the vehicles.

The cowboy said, "Hi, my name is Thomas Blackhawk, welcome to the Rockin' K. I'll be at your disposal while you're here, so feel free to take advantage of that."

Brenda would like to take advantage of him, not the way he meant however, so she told herself to calm down. He didn't have the typical Native American look, in fact she never would have guessed he was Indigenous, but his last name indicated he was. He had light skin and medium brown hair.

Thomas continued, cutting off her wayward thoughts, "These guys are going to help you with the luggage."

Thomas asked Steve and Patricia. "Is there any sensitive equipment in your car that needs to come in out of the cold?"

Patricia answered, "Just a few things. It's all in one bag, each. So, we can take it in easily. All the luggage is in the girls' car."

Thomas walked over to Brenda and asked which luggage went with which person. Brenda could hardly answer, Thomas was even more magnificent up close in a rugged kind of way. His eyes were light brown, almost the color of peanut butter, with gold flecks, they had thick long lashes, that Brenda envied.

Tracy took over for her dumbstruck roommate and pointed out which luggage went with whom.

Thomas gave Steve and Patricia's luggage to two men and said, "Adam's room." The four trooped off.

And then he gave Tracy's luggage to a younger ranch hand that was also good-looking, but didn't hold a candle to Thomas. He said, "Cade's room."

Finally, Thomas himself took Brenda's suitcase. "Follow me."

Brenda did as she was told and was grateful to catch a peek at the man's ass. It was perfect, high and tight in well-fitting jeans. She tried not to fall over her own feet.

When they got almost to the door, a little boy came running out of it and down the few steps in a leap. He looked to be about six or seven, and he ran right up to her and stopped dead. "Are you guys the 'gineers that are going to find what's making a mess up in the northern pasture?"

Brenda squatted down to his height. "Yes, we are. My name is Brenda. What's yours?"

"My name's Tony. I have a new last name. It used to be Kipling. But then, my daddy came back from the rodeo, and Mommy and Daddy got married. And now I have his last name, and it's McCoy. So, I am Tony McCoy. Nice to meet you."

The little guy stuck out his hand and Brenda wanted to laugh, with a quick glance at Thomas who winked at her, she took Tony's little hand and shook it, like he was an adult. "It's very nice to meet you, Tony McCoy. Are you staying in this house too?"

"Yeah, that's my daddy's truck right there, that they're taking all the horses out of. And sometimes we stay in it. But Mama wanted to be by all the family. So, we're staying in the house in our old rooms. Plus, the house is warmer. Daddy's trailer can get a little cold at night, especially up here in the mountains. But we stay in it when Daddy's doing rodeos. Well, Daddy and Mommy are both doing rodeos now. They're team ropers, and they do a really good job."

Brenda wasn't a rodeo fan, so she had no idea what team ropers were, so she said, "I'm sure that they do. It will be very fun to be spending Christmas with you."

"Yeah. Grandpa K said that you guys are going to spend the whole time here with us. But I'm not. After we have Christmas here, we're gonna go and see my grandma, and cousins in Arizona, and have two Christmases."

"Oh, now, that's exciting," Brenda said with another glance at Thomas who was clearly working hard not to laugh at the little boy's zest for life.

The child was practically vibrating with excitement. "Yeah, it is. We do it every year, sometimes we go to Arizona first. But we get to stop at the Great Sand piles, and then go to Emma's Cafe, and they have very fancy breakfast foods, just for me."

"The Great Sand Dunes?" Brenda asked, not quite sure she was following along.

Tony nodded enthusiastically. "Yeah, that's it. Daddy keeps trying to make me remember that, but I keep forgetting. Because to me they're big, giant sand piles."

"Well, yes, they are big giant sand piles, no question about it. But they have an official name, just like you do."

He cocked his head thinking about that.

She chuckled at him, "You like the big sand piles, do you?"

"Oh yes, but I get a little itchy after we get back in the truck. So, we have to stop soon at the hotel. The one we stayed in the first time. It has a swimming pool and Emma's Cafe is right there by it. That's my mommy's name. And that's why we went there the first time. But we get to go back this time, too. They were very nice to me, they gave me ice cream, and made my pancakes look like fishies. It was very fun."

"It sounds like Emma's Cafe must be a wonderful place."

"It is. And the food is so yummy."

Thomas interrupted the child, "Tony, I need to take this suitcase up and show Brenda her room before dinner, so we'll see you a little bit later."

"For dinner! We have a big, big, fancy dinner. At least that's what Nana said."

Thomas nodded. "Well, she would know. So, we'll see you at dinner in just a few minutes."

"Yay."

They left Tony in the yard and went inside. Thomas said, "We'll meet the family in a little bit. We want to get you guys settled before we start the introductions. There's a bunch of Kiplings, so it's gonna take a while. You met the best one out of the whole crew though, just now."

Brenda smiled. "Tony is so cute."

"Yeah, he's a handful, though. Got a lot of personality in that little body."

"Good for him." When they got to her room. She noticed it had an adjoining bathroom with Tracy on the other side. She'd heard that called a Jack and Jill set up.

Thomas set her suitcase on the floor. And she put her purse on the desk. The man filled the space and Brenda wondered where all the air had gone.

Thomas shuffled his feet. "Go ahead and settle in, we won't have dinner for a little bit. They have to finish getting all Zach's horses settled in and fed. About a half an hour, I think."

Brenda swallowed trying to get her voice to work in her throat that was mimicking a desert. "Sounds perfect. Thanks for your help."

Thomas rubbed the back of his neck and she wondered if he was going to say something else. But then he shrugged and walked out the door.

Thomas was going to hell, straight to hell, for having such impure thoughts about that college girl. Now Thomas understood what Zach had gone through, when he'd lusted after Emma while she was in high school and Zach had already graduated. He'd joined the rodeo to keep his hands off of her. Thomas had always thought that was a ridiculous idea. No woman was that irresistible. He no longer had that opinion; he knew exactly how Zach had felt. Brenda had knocked the air right out of him.

He'd almost blurted out how pretty he thought she was, but had managed, with difficulty, to hold his tongue. It was going to be a challenge to work with her for the next three weeks.

He'd felt stupidly possessive when the ranch hands had all stopped working to watch her and the other woman stretch after the long drive. He'd wanted to go all cave man and drag her off, but had instead, assigned the other guys to carry for the other three. Which had probably been a mistake on his part, because of the big bed in her room and his wayward imagination, that had pictured the two of them on that bed, naked.

He was tempted to go dunk his fat head in the ice-cold stock tank, but he knew he'd get confused looks at the dinner table. He'd skip the damn meal if it wasn't a command performance, at least for him. He was the point man for the engineers, so he'd be spending meals with them, as well as all waking hours. Damn.

Thomas decided that the best way to get the woman out of his head was to keep busy. So, he went down to the kitchen, and asked if he could be of service.

Meg looked up from stirring something on the stove.

CHRISTMAS AT THE ROCKIN' K

"Well, most of the food and everything is ready. But you can help get it on the table. Oh no wait, we actually do need a few more chairs, if you could get the folding chairs out of the mudroom."

"That would be perfect. I'll do that. How many do we need?" He asked.

"Just four more. Oh no wait, six more. Since you and Lloyd are going to join us, and the engineers. We've got enough chairs for the family."

"Okay. I'll get them to the table." He was glad Meg had given him something to do that was physical. He didn't just want to stand around, waiting. Waiting gave a person too much thinking time. Better to be working.

He wondered why Lloyd was going to be joining them for dinner. Maybe he was going to be helping with the engineers as well. That might be useful. He wondered how old Brenda was. She was still in college, but she didn't look like she was really young. She was probably a grad student rather than undergrad, which would put her somewhere between twenty-two, and twenty-eight. He was thirty-seven. So maybe not too big of a difference, nine to, damn, fifteen years. Yeah, fifteen was getting up there in the too old category.

He needed to stop thinking about this, it was a stupid idea. And the woman was only gonna be here for three weeks. And then she'd be going back to school. He assumed they'd be sending in a crew to start cleaning up whatever was causing the contamination, it certainly wouldn't be the engineers from the school who would be doing the grunt work. They were here to discover what the problem was, and then turn it over to the people that would do the actual work. At least that was his understanding.

So, he didn't need to be thinking about Brenda as any kind of girlfriend or hookup. Besides, she was way too smart for him, she was going to a school that was prestigious all over the world. He sighed as he went into the mud room, yeah, she was completely out of his league.

He found the chairs he needed and decided to take two trips. He could probably carry all six of them in one trip, but two trips would give him something to do, longer. The longer he was busy, the better. He went into the dining room; the table had been extended. With all of its leaves, it was enormous. With everyone home, and everyone's spouses, and the engineers, they filled the table.

For Christmas, with however many ranch hands were gonna be in at dinner, it wouldn't be a sit-down meal. They wouldn't have enough table space, but Meg had been inviting them all for Christmas dinner for enough years, that she had it down. Everything she made for Christmas was processed or cut up, or whatever, to make it small enough to be finger food.

He didn't know what Meg had cooked for this dinner, or how many of the kids had helped with it. Every single one of the family members knew how to cook. That was one of the things Meg insisted on. And they took turns cooking dinner. There was a chart on the wall, and before all the kids had moved out, every one of their names had been on it rotating for each evening meal. Except during calving season. They didn't put Beau on there because he was the vet. And if something was going on with the cattle he didn't even think about food. So, during calving season they took him off the list.

Thomas put the chairs around the table and went back for the rest. The place setting was already out, so he didn't need to guess where the chairs were needed. Once he set the last three around the table, Travis called him over.

"Since you've met everybody, you can do the introductions."

"Yes sir." Shit. He wasn't looking forward to doing introductions, he didn't like to be center stage. But he *had* met everyone. So, he would do as asked. He decided to wait by the stairs for the engineers to come down and take them to the table.

Meg sent Tony to tell everyone, it was time. He'd taken off running and his voice rang through the halls. "It's time for dinner. It's time for dinner."

Thomas had to laugh at the little guy's enthusiasm. It only took a moment before the guests came down the stairs. His eyes were drawn directly to Brenda, she'd taken her hair out of the ponytail it had been in and it looked soft and inviting. She'd put some makeup on around her eyes, and her mouth was bright red. Lust roared through him.

She was gorgeous in her ponytail with no makeup, now she was just stunning. He wasn't sure he'd be able to speak at all. He heard Lloyd gasp. Thomas turned to give him the evil eye, but Lloyd's attention was not on Brenda. Lloyd's focus was on Tracy. Thomas was relieved that he wouldn't have to punch Lloyd in the face.

Lloyd whispered, "They're beautiful girls."

"Yeah, they are," Thomas agreed. He couldn't deny that they were exceptionally beautiful women, but not for the likes of them. "But way too smart, for the two of us."

Lloyd nodded. But he still stood there, and watched the girls come down the stairs. They were talking to Tony who held their hands. Lucky kid.

Tracy walked right up to Lloyd. And put her hand on his arm. "Are you going to escort me to dinner, kind sir?"

Lloyd laughed. "I would be happy to."

Brenda hesitated a moment, and then followed Tracy's actions. Her small hand rested on his arm and he could swear he felt tingles. It was a stupid thought; he didn't get tingles from a woman's hand on his shirt.

Brenda asked, "Are you going to escort me to dinner, Thomas?"

"Sure thing." He managed to croak out.

It was going to be a long three weeks.

CHAPTER 2

*B*renda had primped. She could admit it, she told herself while she was doing it, it was to make a good impression with the family, but she knew better. She was primping for Thomas. She'd been watching him, when she started down the stairs with Tony, pretending to be talking to the little guy, but in reality, watching Thomas for his reaction.

It had been perfect; he'd looked like he wanted to scoop her right up and carry her off to the nearest bedroom. Maybe she was an idiot for liking that idea, but she'd never felt this way about anyone before. Was this what people called love at first sight? She didn't know if it was love, but it sure was lust at first sight.

There'd been a couple of guys she'd been interested in over the years. She'd had sex, of course, but none of those feelings were anything like the way she was feeling about Thomas.

He was older than her, not by a lot, maybe six or eight years. But that didn't deter her in the least. And he was a cowboy. He wasn't a grad student or an engineer or anything like that. But he was obviously well respected by the family he worked for. And that was all that mattered to her, hardworking and attentive, and he was both.

Even though he was trying to hide his attraction to her she could see it.

She was trying to hide her attraction, too. She would only be here three weeks, it was kind of silly to think about doing anything with Thomas, but three weeks was long enough to scratch an itch. And she had a powerful itch for Thomas.

She'd talked to Tracy for a few minutes before Tony had run through the halls yelling to come have dinner. And apparently, Tracy thought Lloyd was pretty cute. She couldn't deny that he was an attractive man. But Tracy could have him.

The funny thing about all of this was that neither one of them was especially boy crazy. They'd dated here and there, but their main focus was on their education. Was it the fact they were on vacation? Something in the air? The elevation of the ranch might indicate a lack of oxygen. There had to be a reason both she and her roommate were eyeing the men of the Rockin' K.

Brenda had been shocked, when Tracy, bold as brass, had marched up to Lloyd and told him, he was going to escort her into dinner. Brenda never would have thought about doing something like that, but since Tracy had broken the ice, she figured she might as well try, too.

Thomas had looked a little freaked out when she first put her hand on his arm. But then he had graciously taken her into the dining room, that boasted the largest table she'd ever seen, and there wasn't one square inch that wasn't covered.

Once they were all seated, very closely together. Thomas began making introductions. As she looked around the table, she couldn't believe the attractiveness of this family. Clearly, all the Kiplings were gorgeous. The generation that was her age were five men and one woman. But their spouses were just as attractive as they were. She didn't know what kind of genes ran up here, but they were strong.

She'd never keep all of them straight. Well, she might eventually, but not tonight, that was for sure. Thomas had gone around the table in an orderly fashion which helped. But the fact that there was a set of twins made it harder. They looked exactly alike. But when they said hello, it was clear that their personalities were very different.

Cade was super outgoing and teasing about being the best-looking one of the family. Chase had just rolled his eyes at his brother. Both the twins' wives were pregnant, she thought that was rather coincidental. When Thomas had reached Grandpa K in the introductions, she realized where Cade and Tony had gotten their gumption.

Grandpa K had looked at each one of them and had clearly said, "Now, all of you are going to call me Grandpa K. I don't want no 'Mr. Kipling' business. Way too many of us, Mr. Kipling, so I'm Grandpa K. You need any grandfatherly advice you just go ahead and ask. I give very good advice. Don't I?"

The rest of the family laughed and nodded. The man had a twinkle in his eye. And she could see that he'd passed that rascally personality to Cade and then to Tony. Meg, the mother of all the siblings, was a pretty woman and her husband Travis clearly doted on her. Alyssa and Beau, who were introduced as the family veterinarians, had a lovely little girl, Emily, about two years old, who smiled and waved her spoon, when her name was mentioned.

Brenda could see the affection Thomas had for each member of the family as he introduced them. Once the introductions were done, they started passing the food around. It was a feast fit for a king. There were an awful lot of them. So, she imagined it had taken a fair amount of cooking. And she figured some of the daughters-in-law probably had helped prepare the meal.

That assumption, on her part, was confirmed when several of the family members told the different girls how delicious their dish was. Conversations flew across the table between the family members who obviously hadn't seen each other for a while.

Cade teased Emma about having another baby with Zach, while he was awake and aware. Brenda wondered what that was about. Thomas sensed her confusion and whispered, "I'll tell you the story."

"Zach and I are going to wait a couple more years, so we can compete in the rodeo. We still need to get Zach that all-around-cowboy buckle."

Summer said, "Well I hope you have better luck than we did. We didn't plan to get pregnant for another couple of years so we could stay in cheer."

Thomas whispered, "Professional cheerleading, like *Bring it on*."

Her eyebrows rose at that, but Thomas just nodded as the conversation continued.

Cade frowned. "The twin power was too strong for us. It's all Chase's fault for getting Katie preggers. The hormones snuck over to our house."

Chase shrugged. "We've done every other single thing at the same time, why would having a baby be different?"

Katie said, "If you don't mind my asking, Patricia, when are you due?"

Brenda watched in awe as her, hard core, tough as nails, female engineer, professor, blushed prettily. Brenda had known Dr. Patricia was pregnant, she had eyes, but she'd never heard it mentioned. "The baby is due in March, just about the same time as the energy summit that brought Steve back to Colorado. He will not be the keynote speaker this year, and neither one of us are planning to teach classes for the event."

Grandpa K chuckled, "Good plan, those young'uns like to come at the least perfect time. Just ask Beau and Alyssa."

Everyone groaned, Alyssa and Beau did not offer illumination. Thomas said, "Alyssa's water broke right in the middle of a difficult birth. Fortunately, they got the calf born and were on the way to Granby in time to make it to the hospital. We told Beau that everyone of us could help with a home birth, women weren't all that different from cattle. Beau looked a little pale at the suggestion, and he insisted his baby would be in the hospital and delivered by the OB/GYN and not by his idiot brothers or ranch hands."

Chuckles wound around the table and the talk moved on to ranching subjects.

Brenda enjoyed hearing the chitchat of the family. Thomas interjected his comments on some of the discussion, often just to her, which made her feel special. Her family was so reserved and boring, that listening to this huge group was quite a change. Her family during dinner time had been for eating. Not talking, of course it was just her and her parents. So, if she didn't want to get the third degree, she kept silent.

Her parents split when she'd graduated from high school. Even before that they had lived in separate rooms of the house, separate wings actually. Her mom had one wing and her dad had the other. Dinner was the only time they all came together, a civilized time of cohabitation.

Her parents didn't really fight, they just didn't care about each other. And she never really felt loved either. They were cold people. Nothing like this rowdy, loving family.

When everyone had eaten most of their meal, Travis

cleared his throat, and the room became silent. "I want to thank you, Dr. Patricia, Professor Steve, Brenda, and Tracy, for spending your winter break with us. Hopefully we can figure out where the contamination is coming from and determine a solution."

He looked around the table as everyone nodded but kept silent. "The reason I've asked Thomas to work with you is because he is a mighty fine tracker. And he might be able to help you track the contamination back to its source. If anyone can do it, it will be him. He may not look like a Ute Mountain Native American, but the genes are still there."

"Along with very detailed education on the subject by both my father and grandfather," Thomas said.

Brenda took that to mean that Thomas didn't want them to think he was acting on gut instinct, but instead on training. She was glad she'd been right about assuming he was Native American based on his last name.

Travis continued, "Since you tested the samples we sent, and think it is contamination from an old gold mine, I asked Lloyd to help you as well. His father had an interest in gold mines, and they did a little bit of work at one of them, when Lloyd was a teenager. Of course, the methods used even fifteen years ago were different from the olden days. Regardless, I thought he could be of assistance as well."

Steve nodded. "Sounds like we've got a good crew then. We'll start first thing in the morning, by going out and looking at the area. Brenda is my grad student intern. She'll be graduating with her doctorate in the spring. Tracy is Patricia's grad student, and she's got another year to go before she graduates with her doctorate. Both the ladies will benefit from working on this project."

Steve's eyes twinkled. "And frankly, I don't know what I

would do without Brenda most of the time, and I'm pretty sure Patricia feels the same way about Tracy."

Brenda was both pleased and embarrassed by the comments Steve was making.

Travis asked, "Do all of you ride horses? The mountains can be difficult to traverse in vehicles sometimes. We were thinking to stable some horses out by cabin two, which is at the north end of the ranch up where we're finding the contamination. And that way if you need to continue on a path that is not vehicle friendly you can take horses."

Brenda had gone through a horse loving stage at one point. And her parents had allowed her to take riding lessons. They'd been in a flat arena riding around and around, however, not traipsing through the mountains.

She said, "I've ridden, but not that kind of riding. We didn't live near mountains or any kind of rural area. We mostly lived in Manhattan. My parents indulged my love of horses, by taking me to a riding club where we rode around in an arena."

Travis nodded. "Yeah, not quite the same."

Tracy said, "I rode a couple of times in summer camps, when my foster families ditched me to go on family vacations. But it wasn't often or strenuous riding."

Patricia and Steve nodded with Tracy. Steve said, "Yeah. Us too. We've done a little bit of riding but nothing significant. We'll probably need to be on foot the first day or two as we take samples from the contaminated area. First order of business is to determine the contamination field and the direction it's coming from."

"All right. Hopefully, you can get comfortable, once you're ready to use the horses." Travis looked at Thomas. "Gentle mounts that are obedient."

Thomas nodded. "Yep. What time do you folks want to start in the morning?"

Steve said, "Early. Nine o'clock."

Brenda noticed nearly everyone around the table trying to hide a smirk. Nine o'clock, was clearly not an early start on a cattle ranch.

Thomas didn't miss a beat and said, "That's perfect. The sun'll be up by then. We'll take the vehicles to cabin two, and then set out from there. You can take your equipment and leave it in the cabin, while we go searching."

"Sounds good."

Meg said, "There'll be breakfast in the kitchen with plenty of coffee. Feel free to help yourselves."

MANHATTAN? BRENDA WAS FROM NEW YORK CITY AND HAD enjoyed riding lessons in the area. Thomas didn't know for certain, but living in Manhattan had to be expensive, and riding lessons even more so. He had a very bad feeling he was lusting after a very rich woman. Her car would indicate that also, he didn't think most college students drove a Range Rover Defender, and by the looks of it, it was only a couple of years old.

Shit. He was a ranch hand, sure he made decent money, and most of that went into the bank because his pay included housing, but he wouldn't be buying a Range Rover any time soon.

So now she was maybe six years younger than he was. A helluva lot smarter than he was. And rich, maybe a trust fund baby. Well damn, it just keeps getting worse and worse, while the attraction soared. He'd observed her watching the interactions at the dinner table and her reactions had been similar to his own. Of course, he knew the family, so he understood the jokes and teasing, but Brenda seemed to catch on quickly.

She had to have some flaws. He was going to keep his eyes peeled to find out what those were, so he could concentrate on those things, not all the delightful aspects of her personality. And he wasn't even going to let himself think about her physical attractions, no those were already screaming high. Nope, no dwelling on her golden blonde hair and violet eyes, on her upturned nose with, dear God, freckles, and her wide, made for kissing mouth. Her slight frame had just the right amount of curves and were off-limit thoughts, too.

He needed a distraction, now. He cleared his throat, "If I'm not needed any longer, I have some stuff to do."

Meg frowned. "We still have dessert and it's one of your favorites, apple pie a la mode."

He did love Meg's apple pie, but he just couldn't stand sitting next to Brenda for one moment longer. "I'd be obliged if you saved me a piece, but I really need to get going, to, um, finish up tonight, so I can spend tomorrow with our guests."

Meg said, "By all means, I'll send a piece for you with Lloyd."

"Thanks, now if you will all excuse me, I'll meet you in the yard at nine tomorrow." As he stood, he noticed a look of confusion on both Travis and Lloyd's faces. They both knew he wasn't working on anything significant. Travis had deliberately taken him off the duty list so he would have the time to assist the engineers.

He stomped out to the barn cussing himself for being an idiot. He wasn't a teenage boy who couldn't control himself around a pretty girl. For that matter he couldn't remember acting this way when he *had* been a teenager.

He yanked open the barn door. Surely, he could find

something to keep him occupied, there were always chores needing to be done on a cattle ranch. He checked on Zach's horses to make sure they were content in their stalls. Zach had mentioned one of them had gotten hurt and spent the last few weeks at the horse rescue ranch in Wyoming, where Drew's wife, Lily, worked.

When he went into that stall, he noticed the horse still seemed to be favoring his sore leg. Another three weeks healing might help, but Thomas didn't think that horse would be competing again any time soon, if ever. That might be why Lily's family was coming in tomorrow rather than today, because they were bringing a replacement for Zach.

If anyone could get the horse healed up it would be Beau and Alyssa. The Rockin' K was lucky to have two superior veterinarians in the family. He guessed they'd be taking this horse to their house and stabling him in the enormous clinic they'd built on Beau's land.

Thomas looked in on the rest of the horses, they all looked perfectly content and none of them needed his attention. He wandered over to the cattle side of the barn. There were only a few animals in there and none of them seemed the least bit interested in him.

He looked into the tack room, but everything was orderly there and nothing needed repairs except one saddle, and he knew they were waiting for a shipment to repair it. Finally giving up, he went to his room in the bunk house, and flopped down on his bed, calling himself an idiot, and vowing to keep himself under better control. He wasn't a damn teenager.

CHAPTER 3

A knock came on the door to the bathroom, which meant Tracy.

"Enter," Brenda said.

Tracy walked in with her backpack and coat. "That response to my knock makes me feel like a peasant, and you are the mighty queen summoning her servant."

Brenda laughed. "Then my goal has been accomplished."

"You're just silly."

Brenda beamed. "I am. But that's why you love me."

Tracy shook her head. "Right. You ready?"

"Yep." She put the last item in her backpack and grabbed a coat. "Do you have your gloves and hat and stuff?" Brenda asked.

"Sure do. The last thing I want to do is get cold."

"Right? It's probably going to be frigid up here in the mountains. The weather app said they were predicting snow for this evening."

Tracy sighed. "Yeah, I saw that, too. The question is will it be an inch, or will it be a yard? It could go either way up here."

"True that. So, let's see if we can't put a dent in what we need to do before that weather blows in, because we might not be able to do anything afterwards."

"Yeah. But if we can get a solid eight hours, it should give us a decent path to look at on the maps tonight. Or even tomorrow if we need to."

Brenda opened the door to her room that led out into the hall. "Exactly. Let's go get breakfast."

"I hope there's coffee, I think I smell coffee."

"Yeah, I do, too," Brenda said.

Brenda turned off the light in the bedroom and they trooped down the stairs to the kitchen, where they did indeed smell coffee, as well as all kinds of other delightful scents when they walked in the kitchen.

Patricia and Steve were already there with plates full of delicious looking food.

Brenda marched right over to the coffee and got herself a big mug of it, put a tiny bit of sugar in, stirred it up, and took her first drink. "Ah, now I'll wake up."

Patricia said, "Well while you're waking up, get some food. We've got about forty-five minutes before we're going to leave."

Brenda set her coffee cup down on the table, after one more sip of the life-giving elixir, and went over to the food that was in warming dishes. She flipped up the lid, there was still plenty of food left. The first one held oatmeal with bowls of brown sugar, raisins, and nuts. She wasn't a huge fan of oatmeal, so she moved on.

There were scrambled eggs with bacon and chives, and also plain scrambled eggs. Then another warmer that had bacon, sausage links, and slices of ham. Next were hash browns, some doctored with chives and cheese, and some plain. The next warmer had cinnamon rolls that look to be homemade.

There was enough food there for thirty people. She'd never seen so many choices in a home. Restaurants or fundraisers, sure, but a home? Of course, she didn't know who had eaten and who hadn't. Some of them probably did chores before they ate breakfast. At the very end was, surprisingly enough, cereal with bowls. Rice Krispies in fact, it seemed a little odd to her, but to each his own.

She didn't want to eat too much and be sluggish all day, so she selected some of the already-doctored eggs, then took a cinnamon roll and a fat chunk of butter. There were two types of juices as well, apple and orange, but she decided she didn't need juice, she would have coffee instead.

Tracy had gone for the plain eggs, a little bit of each one of the meats, with toast and a glass of apple juice.

"No cinnamon roll for you, Tracy?" Patricia asked.

"Well, they are tempting, but I don't know, I wanted to have more protein for the day ahead."

Steve nodded. "That's probably a good choice. Maybe you could take a cinnamon roll for later. Or even put one up in your room for tonight."

Tracy's eyes lit up. "Oh, that's a good idea."

Steve chuckled. "I was thinking about doing it myself. With a big slab of butter."

Patricia rolled her eyes. "You're incorrigible."

"I know, that's why you love me," Steve laughed.

Brenda wondered if she'd gotten that phrase from him or he'd gotten it from her. Clearly, they were spending too much time together.

They all started tucking into their food, drinking their coffee, and talking about the plans for the day.

"Thomas is going to take us to where they first noticed

the contamination and show us the area they cordoned off, that they think is fully contaminated," Steve said.

Thomas's name sent Brenda spinning back to his quick exit last night. She'd been both relieved and disappointed when he'd left so abruptly, she'd had trouble focusing with him sitting right next to her. Several of the Kiplings had exchanged glances, she hadn't known what that was about, and they hadn't mentioned it. But clearly something was unexpected about his departure. She pushed her thoughts to the side, as the plans for the day continued.

Patricia and Tracy were going to take rock samples and do a quick survey of the area, while Steve and Brenda took soil and plant samples to run through their portable lab equipment later tonight.

Brenda got up to refill her coffee. "Anybody else want some?" She shook the pot.

Tracy called out, "I do."

"Sure," said Steve.

Patricia nodded.

Brenda filled up everyone's cup, brought the sugar and a little pitcher of milk over to the table, as well as the nondairy creamer. It was fun for her to be able to serve others, she'd always been the one being served.

Steve took a long drink then said, "I think it would be easiest to take Patricia's car. That way all the equipment will be in there. And we won't have to switch it around. The five of us, I mean the six of us, can squeeze in for that long of a drive."

Thomas spoke from the doorway. "That won't be necessary. It'll just be five of us, Lloyd is going to take the horses up to cabin two, then he'll ride one over and join us, once he gets them settled. I've already got a thermos of coffee to take with us to warm us up during the day. If the weather comes in early, we'll knock off and come back to the ranch house."

Brenda's heart had leapt when Thomas appeared in the doorway. He'd quickly glanced at her, and then studiously kept his eyes on Steve. Had she seen a flicker of light in his eyes when he'd looked at her? For a moment before he'd steeled his expression and looked away? She certainly hoped so.

Steve said, "Perfect." Brenda fought to remember what they'd been talking about as Steve continued, "We can leave the cold sensitive equipment here. It's to test the rocks, soil, and grass. So, we'll just take some samples, carefully document the locations, and bring them back here to test."

Thomas nodded. "Good, I was going to have you store it in the cabin and keep the heat up in there. But if we don't need to, that's even easier."

"No need for that. At least not today. We might want to bring it out later as we follow the trail."

They finished their coffee, rinsed out their cups and their plates, and put them in the dishwasher.

Tracy glanced longingly at the cinnamon rolls.

Brenda asked Thomas. "Is there something Tracy could take one of those cinnamon rolls in?'

"Sure, we've got some plastic containers she can put one in. I'll go get it," Thomas said.

Steve piped up, "Get two if you don't mind."

Thomas just laughed as he went into what Brenda assumed was the pantry. When he came out, he had *three* containers. He gave one to Tracy, one to Steve, and took one for himself. But in his, he put a cinnamon roll, four strips of bacon, and two sausage links.

Then he looked around and said, "I'm a growing boy."

They all laughed. Steve and Tracy put theirs in their backpacks, and Thomas carried his out to the mud room, where he put back on his boots and coat, then grabbed his own backpack, where he put his container. "Okay, let's head out there, is everybody ready? Anyone need to use the bathroom or anything first? We won't be around any facilities."

Patricia raised an eyebrow. "Hey, we're engineers. We know how to use the woods."

"Fair enough."

They put their backpacks in the hatch, and Steve drove. Thomas navigated, and the three women were in the backseat. Fortunately, the Rav4 had plenty of space in the backseat, especially leg room. It took about twenty minutes to get to cabin two, which Thomas pointed out. And then they went further north and west across the pasture.

Thomas said, "The grass is a little longer than normal, because we had to shut the pasture up until you guys got out here. We would have normally had the cattle up here as the last location before winter and when we bring them in closer."

The drive was a little bumpy but not nearly as bad as Brenda had thought it would be.

When Steve stopped the vehicle, they were at the foot of some hills.

"We think that this is where the contamination is coming from." Thomas pointed up a narrow ravine. "There's a stream that runs down through there. So, we think it's coming from there. We could be wrong of course, there's little streams like that all over, where the pasture meets the mountains."

"It's as good a place as any to start," Steve said.

"Yeah, that's what I thought too."

Patricia pushed open her door. "Okay, let's get to checking stuff out."

They all clambered out of the vehicle and went around to

the back to grab their backpacks and the equipment that they were going to need to start.

When Lloyd arrived, Thomas assigned him to work with the mine reclamation engineers, Steve, and Brenda, and he went to help Patricia, and Tracy. That way he would avoid temptation with Brenda, and Lloyd knew more about mines than he did.

They worked separately until lunch and then gathered back at the SUV to share what they'd discovered. They'd made a little bit of progress, at least Patricia and Steve thought so. They were narrowing down the direction they felt was the most likely. They agreed with Thomas's idea that it was probably coming from the ravine they were next to, but they wouldn't know for sure until they'd tested the samples.

After the lunch that Meg had packed for them, they went back to work. A few hours later, the temperature plummeted. It was colder than it had been all day, and the wind had picked up. A sure sign that snow was on its way. Thomas went to gather everyone up so they could get moving before the snow started in earnest. There were already a few flakes swirling in the wind. Nothing significant, but that could change in ten minutes.

He told his team to head to the vehicle and not to tarry and went to find the environmental engineers. He saw Steve and Lloyd, but not Brenda.

He said, "Where's Brenda?"

Steve looked around. "Oh, um, well the last thing she said was that she was going to go find a bush."

"Okay. When was that?"

Steve frowned. "A while ago actually, she should have been back by now."

They quickly scoured the area, but she was nowhere to be found.

Thomas wanted to smack someone, but said, "All the rest of you take the Rav4 back to the ranch. Lloyd, go with them. You can direct them back. I'll take your horse back to cabin two once I find Brenda. If the weather holds, you can come get us, if it doesn't, we'll hunker down in the cabin. I'll let you know."

He needed to find the woman asap, he hoped she wasn't hurt or lost. He didn't want her to get cold or have the snow cover her tracks. "You guys go ahead and go, so I can get started tracking her."

He hoped it wouldn't take him very long, she couldn't have gone too far, could she? He quickly found the place where she'd used the facilities, so to speak. Then tracked her farther north. He didn't know why exactly she was going north but she was, even though they'd been working to the south.

He followed her trail over a mile north. Where in the hell was she headed? But she wasn't doubling back or wandering around. He did find evidence of her scratching at the rocks. He kept tracking her as the snow started coming down harder, fortunately not obscuring her trail, yet. Another mile and he saw her up ahead with a branch.

He rushed up. "What happened?"

"Oh, thank God." She leaned on him. "I twisted my ankle. So, I was looking around for this lovely branch to hold on to. I finally found one and was about to text you guys to come get me when a freaking bear walked out of the woods. Scared the crap out of me and my phone went flying. But I stood still like you're supposed to, you know."

CHRISTMAS AT THE ROCKIN' K

She sighed. "I didn't see where it landed, and I couldn't move anyway waiting for the bear to move on. So, I was just standing here. It did cross my mind to hit it over the head with the branch, but I figured that was a sure-fire way to be his dinner."

Thomas felt his blood run cold to think of her whacking a bear with a stick when she had a bad ankle.

She shivered and he wondered if it was from the cold or latent fear. "So, I was just waiting for him to go. Then he goes over and sits down and starts eating off this one bush. I don't know what it was exactly, it might have been blackberries it looked kinda blackberry-ish. So, he's munching away while I'm standing still. My ankle is throbbing, I'm getting colder, and then I see a few flakes. And I'm just standing there like a dumb ass." Her voice had gotten shriller toward the end of the story and he feared she was getting shocky.

Thomas chuckled nervously and tried to sooth her. "No, you weren't standing there like a dumb ass, you were standing there, intelligently not moving."

"Well, still, I was irritated. Finally, the stupid bear gets up and wanders off. So, I can start searching for my phone. I had just found it and was hobbling over to get it when you walked out of the trees."

"So where is it?"

"Right there." She pointed.

He saw her phone, laying between a couple of rocks with some grass around it making it damn hard to see.

He grabbed the phone and gave it to her. "I'm gonna carry you back to where we were working, and then we'll take the horse back to the cabin. Lloyd can come get us providing the weather holds."

Just then, a flurry of snow fell, he had a bad feeling about this. "We need to hurry. We can spend the night in cabin two, but it would be better to get back to the ranch." Shit that's all he needed was to spend the night alone with Brenda in a tiny cabin. Temptation on a stick.

Brenda shivered. "I agree. I'm ready to go. I got kind of cold from standing there waiting for that stupid bear to go."

"Okay, I'm going to put you over my shoulder and I'm going to be moving quickly so your ankle might hurt some, but it's better than getting stuck out here in a blizzard."

"I'm right with you. Are you sure I'm not going to be too heavy? I can try…" She tried to take a step and he could see the pain in her face.

He shook his head. "Absolutely not. You probably don't weigh as much as a bag of feed or two."

"All right, let's go."

He hoisted her up over his shoulder and he took off at a fast walk. Her sweet derriere was right there by his face. They needed to get moving for more than just the snow. He knew where he was going, so he hustled along as fast as he could without jostling her too much. Fortunately, it didn't take them long to get back to the horse, but the snow was coming down harder and harder.

The horse looked mighty relieved when they showed up and nickered at him as if to say, "It's about time dude, get me out of this shit." He put Brenda as far forward in the saddle as she could get and then climbed on behind her. Which meant he had to reach around her for the reins, her soft breasts brushing his arms, her ass up close and personal with his crotch.

The horse was more than ready to go back to the barn, so didn't need much encouragement. Thank God, he didn't need to have his arms around Brenda, any longer than was absolutely necessary. By the time they got to the cabin it was nearly white out conditions. Not quite, he could still see through it, which meant he could find the cabin. But it was damn close. He stopped by the porch of cabin and let her down, which made him feel strangely bereft of her presence.

He groaned at himself inwardly. "Do you think you can get inside, while I go put the horse in the barn?"

Her teeth were chattering but she said, "Yeah, I think so."

"Text Steve while you're in there and tell him we're going to stay here at cabin two. Have him tell Lloyd, not to come out in this."

"Okay."

Thomas took the horse over to the barn, pulled the tack off, rubbed him down, fed all the horses, made sure they had water and went back to the cabin. He was damn glad he knew where the cabin was, because he sure as hell couldn't see it. Fortunately, his sense of direction was highly attuned, and he made it to the cabin door and pushed it open, then slammed it shut, as snow swirled into the cabin. Brenda was sitting right inside the door on one of the kitchen chairs.

"I made it this far, but decided I better sit for a minute."

He took his coat off and hung it up. "Let me take a look at your ankle."

"Do you think it's a good idea to take off the boot?"

"Yeah, we need to look at it."

"But it will swell more."

"Nothing we can do about that." He dropped down and started untying the laces as gently as he could.

She hissed. "I really think it's just sprained. I've had a break before, and it doesn't feel like a break. I've had a sprain a time or two and that's what it feels like."

"Good. But let's just check anyway, then we can wrap it. We keep first aid kits in all the cabins." He pulled the boot off as gently as he could, and she still let out a whimper.

That sound tore into him, but he had to continue, he

pulled the sock down as gently as possible, and looked at her small narrow foot. He gently felt her foot up to her ankle, he didn't feel any looseness in the bones. He didn't know for sure, of course, because he didn't have an x-ray machine.

But he was going to take her word for it, that it really just was a sprain, because he couldn't feel anything that might indicate otherwise. He got the first aid kit out, found an ace bandage and wrapped her ankle with it. Then he mashed up the ice pack, so that it would get cold, brought another kitchen chair over and propped her leg on it. Then he grabbed a kitchen towel and draped it and the cold bag over her ankle.

"Will you be okay for a minute so I can get the fire started?'

"Yes, but can you get me a glass of water so I can take some ibuprofen?"

"Sure thing. There's a bottle right there in the first aid kit."

"Yeah, I see it."

He grabbed a bottle of water out of the pantry and gave it to her. Since they'd known they'd be using the cabin this week they'd filled up the refrigerator and the pantry. Made sure they had plenty of food and bread, all the perishable items they might need, that they didn't leave in the cabins year-round. The cabins were always stocked with emergency supplies and food.

He went over and started a fire in the fireplace, and a fire in the wood burning stove.

"I would have taken the ibuprofen, in my backpack if that stupid bear hadn't arrived, but I didn't think I should be digging around in my backpack, while the bear was sitting there having his lunch."

He chuckled. He marveled at her calm and he wondered if

she was in shock or if she simply had a strong personality. "No, that's probably a good thing that you didn't."

"But then once I got in the cabin door, I dropped it, my backpack, over there by the door, rather than bringing it with me so that I could take it. Idiot."

He didn't like her calling herself that, so he said, "It's okay, it was just a few minutes."

"Yeah, but it hurts," her voice shook.

"I know it does. Let me get some dinner whipped up, and then I'll carry you over to the couch where you can be more comfortable."

"Oh, okay," she sniffed.

He wanted to hold her and give her comfort and kisses, but he didn't trust himself one tiny bit. "We've got plenty of food to choose from, steak, Italian, Mexican. Is there anything specific you want?"

"Chicken noodle soup if you've got it. That's what I eat when I need comfort, and I need comfort."

He crouched down in front of her and took her hands in his. "You did everything exactly right. I know your ankle hurts, but we're safe and warm here in the cabin, and we have plenty of food. So, there's nothing to worry about."

She didn't look convinced, but she nodded, so he stood and went into the pantry. He came out with two cans of chicken noodle soup. "I'll just heat these up. There's plenty more in there if you need more."

"Well, I shouldn't need more tonight."

"No, probably not. I'm going to make you a salad to go with it. And some biscuits."

"Wow. A gourmet chicken soup dinner."

She had a strange definition of gourmet, but he winked at her. "I can even make brownies for dessert if you want."

That got a laugh out of her and he felt ten feet tall.

CHAPTER 4

*B*renda's emotions were a mess. She was sitting in a cabin, safe, warm, her leg propped up with ice on it, Ibuprofen in her system, and a sexy man making her dinner. Everything looked perfect. She'd survived a bear encounter, she'd found her phone, Thomas had rescued her. Everything was good, but her emotions were running wild.

She was good at hiding them. She'd learned the hard way, as a child, to hide her emotions. So, she looked all stoic on the outside, but on the inside? Yeah, not so good. She'd been terrified. She'd been hurt. She'd been worried. She'd been scared, she was all alone. What if no one came to find her? She knew she could hobble back to the car, but any further than that and she'd be lost.

Brenda had forced those feelings away while the trouble was at hand. But now that she was sitting, warm in the cabin, safe, and taken care of, those emotions were forcing their way back to her consciousness. Whirling inside her, jumping around like a bunch of crazy toddlers. She couldn't let them out of course. She could barely acknowledge them. Because if she did, she might fall apart, and that would get ugly.

CHRISTMAS AT THE ROCKIN' K

There was no way in hell she was going to fall apart in front of Thomas. So, she forced them down again. Locked them deep away, so she could sit there calmly and watch the man make her dinner. He wasn't doing anything crazy, opening a couple of cans of soup and pouring it into a pan to put on the burner. Adding some milk to the biscuit mix, sliding the dropped biscuits into the oven, and chopping up some veggies to add to the bag of salad. Nothing earth shattering but it made her want to sob, cry like a baby. Clearly her emotions were still raging.

Maybe if she focused on how sexy he looked in the kitchen. When he went over to look in the refrigerator, she focused on how well his jeans fit his ass as he bent to look in. He turned and caught her staring; she felt her face heat.

"What kind of salad dressing do you want? It looks like we have ranch, thousand island, Italian, and blue cheese."

"Ranch is fine."

He grabbed the ranch out of the refrigerator and brought it and the salad over to the table already divided into two big pasta bowls. "Go ahead and get started I'm just going to give the soup a quick stir and then I'll join you. The biscuits need another five minutes, so that should give the soup enough time to be hot." He stirred the soup.

While she doctored her salad with dressing and a few croutons, he found butter, honey, and a small jar of grape jelly, and brought that over and set it on the table along with some crackers. She didn't think she'd need crackers if they were having biscuits, but it was thoughtful of him to put them out.

He gave the soup one more stir, and asked her what she wanted to drink. "Looks like we've got several different kinds of soda. Iced tea, both sweet and unsweetened, water of course, and some different juices, apple, cranberry, orange, and grape.

She felt a little shaky so she went with juice, she wasn't a pop drinker, but she felt like she could use some sugar. "Apple juice, I think. I'm feeling a little shaky and the sugar would probably help."

A look of horror came over his features. "Oh shit, of course you are. I didn't even think about the adrenaline rush you must have had. Here I am playing Betty Crocker and your blood sugar is plummeting." He grabbed a glass, put some ice into it and filled it to the top with apple juice.

She took a healthy swallow.

"Don't wait for me, go ahead and start eating your salad."

She did as she was told, while he dished up the rest. Thomas joined her a few minutes later with bowls of steaming soup and delicious-looking biscuits. She ate every bite of her salad and pushed her bowl into the center of the table, and pulled her soup in close, letting the steam waft over her. She drew in a deep breath and felt herself calm.

While she waited for her soup to cool, she took a biscuit, split it open, and slathered butter on it, then added some honey. The first bite made her hum with pleasure. "These are delicious."

"Thanks, I worked really hard pouring in the milk and stirring." He grinned at her and she felt her heart flutter, he was so good looking, she wanted to lap him up right along with her soup.

She laughed, "Don't forget dropping spoonfuls onto the pan and putting them in the oven."

"Can't forget that. I've been slaving away in the kitchen, opening cans, stirring milk, chopping up veggies." He pretended to wipe sweat off his brow.

She cracked up and he grinned like she'd just given him

the greatest gift. Then she took a bite of her soup and moaned in appreciation. She knew it was canned soup, but it hit the spot. With each bite of her go-to comfort food, she was soothed and became calmer and more in control. She wasn't fighting her feelings as much as she had been.

Brenda looked up at him. "This is exactly what I needed."

"I aim to serve."

When she'd eaten three biscuits, her whole bowl of soup, and her whole salad, she felt like she might explode. "That was the best meal ever. Thank you so much for making it for me. I ate way too much. But it was so delicious, and it did exactly what it was supposed to do, get some food into me, as well as a whole bunch of calm."

He chuckled. "Glad to hear it. I'm happy to make you food. How about I carry you over and you can stretch out on the couch. Maybe lie down and let your foot be elevated. It will help with the throbbing, which I'm sure you're feeling."

She didn't deny that she felt throbbing. The idea of laying down sounded wonderful. "That would be perfect. Thanks."

He came around the table, picked her up, like she weighed nothing, and carried her over to the couch. He set her down gently, put a pillow under her foot, and another pillow under her head, grabbed an Afghan, and laid it over her. "Now you just rest while I clean up the kitchen."

"Yes sir."

He winked at her. "That's what I like to hear. Obedience."

She stuck her tongue out at him. He laughed and walked back into the kitchen.

She let herself fully relax, warm, cozy, and full.

∼

Thomas hurried back to the kitchen before he acted on impulse. That pink tongue had sent him spinning into forbidden territory. He could think of several places she could use it on his body, slowly. He put the brakes on his thoughts and forced them away by concentrating on the tasks at hand. Clean the kitchen, find the 'girl box', check the bedrooms, make brownies, anything else he could think of to keep his mind away from Brenda and her tongue.

Thomas cleaned up the kitchen. When he was finished, he went over to check on Brenda. She was sound asleep. Which was probably good for her, so he left her to rest. She'd had quite an ordeal and sleep was good for healing, both physically and emotionally.

He decided that he was going to whip up those brownies. It might be good to have a snack for later, and the smell of chocolate baking would wake her up gently. He didn't know a woman alive that would sleep through that, most men, neither. She might still need a few more calories or a little bit more carbs, to make up for the trauma that she'd been through.

He got the box out of the pantry and put in the water, oil, and egg that they needed, stirred them up and popped them into the oven. Then he went to go find the 'girl basket' that Lily and Alyssa had put together for each one of the cabins.

When Drew had found Lily and had brought her back to this cabin, because of her fear of anyone finding her, all they'd had in the cabin was men-sized clothing. Lily was not a big person. She'd been swimming in those clothes. After that, she and Alyssa had vowed that they would make sure each cabin could handle a female guest.

He found the pink container and peeked inside. There was a pair of sweats, medium-sized, they still might swim on Lily and Brenda, but at least they weren't men's. Red flannel pajamas caught his eye, perfect for the week before Christmas.

Thomas didn't delve any deeper, not wanting to know what might be lurking further down. He didn't need to see strange, mystical female products. Leaving the bin on the floor next to her, he went off to scout himself some clothes.

What he found made him smile, there were red flannel pajamas for men that nearly matched the ones for Brenda. They could match, not that he'd be wearing the shirt. He couldn't sleep in a shirt; it drove him crazy. He laughed and figured it would be funny if they wore matching pajamas.

The cabin could sleep eight, ten in a crunch. There were four bunk beds and two double beds. The bunk beds were in one room and the double beds in the second room. The couch also folded out, but he hated trying to sleep on a hideaway bed, the support bars always hit the wrong places. So, he didn't add that to his sleeping comfortably total for the cabin. In his opinion, it didn't count.

He would give Brenda the double bedroom and he'd take the bunk beds. Fortunately, they were oversized bunk beds, so that a man could actually sleep in them comfortably. Thomas got her room ready, turned down the sheets, so that when he carried her in, he could just put her right into the bed, and quickly leave. He did not want to think about her in that bed. There would be no lingering in her room once he'd brought her in. Nope, he needed to make a quick getaway.

Once he had the rooms ready, he went back out into the common area, and could smell the brownies. Apparently, Brenda could smell the brownies too, because he heard her moving around on the couch.

He peered over the back. "Need some help?"

She grimaced. "Yeah, if you could help me sit up that

would be wonderful. It's hard to maneuver with one foot propped up."

With a chuckle, he put his hands under her armpits and pulled her up into a sitting position. A couple of pillows behind her back helped keep her upright. Then he fixed the pillow under her foot. "How's the ankle?"

"Still hurts but not as bad. I smell chocolate."

"Yes, you do. I made brownies."

Brenda groaned. "Oh man, I'm going to weigh a thousand pounds, just from today."

"No, you're not. Don't be silly. You used up way more calories being terrified and standing there perfectly still watching that bear."

"Yeah, I've got to admit that's true. And hoping and praying someone would show up, but not until after the bear left."

Thomas chuckled. "Yeah, that might not have been fun if I had just marched into the clearing with the bear still there. I am pretty observant, so I probably would have noticed him. Or at least wondered why you were standing perfectly still."

"Good to know for the next time. Dear God, please don't let there be a next time."

"There shouldn't be a next time, I don't know why that bear was still out rummaging about, they are usually deep in hibernation by now."

"That is a question. Stupid bear."

"So now that you've had a little nap. Do you want to read? Or there are some games here. Cards, Yahtzee, chess."

"Well, after we have brownies, let's play chess. I love it."

He wanted to groan. Of course, she loved it. She'd probably kick his ass. It wasn't his favorite game, and she was a whole hell of a lot smarter than he was. Yep, he was gonna have his ass handed to him. That was for sure. But if it would keep her mind occupied and help pass the time. That would be good, too.

"What's this pink bucket?"

"That's the 'girl's box', it should have anything you could possibly need to spend a night or two here in the cabin."

"Really?"

"Yeah, Drew's wife, Lily... Well, it's a long story, but let's just say she ended up in this cabin with no supplies whatsoever. And not one thing in here fit her."

"She is kind of tiny."

"Yes. And everything we had in here was for men. Drew found some sweats, but she still was swallowed up by them. After that, Alyssa and Lily stocked each cabin with a girl's box."

"Ooh, I can hardly wait to rifle through it."

"Well, you go ahead and look through it while I take the brownies out of the oven."

She rubbed her hands together. "Okay."

He pulled it over closer to her so that she could reach it and went into the kitchen.

CHAPTER 5

*B*renda rifled through the "girl box". It had sweats and pajamas, hair and bath products, anti-perspirant, a hairbrush, toothbrushes and toothpaste, various hair ties, and other feminine products including tampons, and surprisingly enough, condoms. Apparently, the women didn't take any chances. She wondered what exactly had taken place in this cabin to have that be a necessary item. She wouldn't mind using them... if Thomas was interested.

While she brushed her hair and put it back into a ponytail, she thought about their plans for the evening. She was happy to play chess, but what she'd really like to do is ask Thomas about a million questions. Maybe she could sneak them in while they played. She'd not had the energy to ask earlier but she did now. The food and rest had helped a lot.

She was clutching the pajamas when Thomas came back in. "Would you like to change into those?"

"Only enough to beg."

"No begging required." He picked her up again as if she was light as a feather. "Do you need anything else out of the box? I can put it in your room."

"That would be great. Too bad there aren't some crutches hanging about, then you wouldn't have to carry me."

"I didn't even look," he said, "but, I don't mind carrying you."

"I'm kind of surprised at how well the cabins are stocked, even with a Christmas tree."

He chuckled, "That's Meg's doing. She doesn't want anyone not having festive decorations if they get stuck in one of the cabins this time of year."

"That's so sweet of her."

"I suppose, it seems like a lot of work for cabins that might not even be occupied."

He set her in the bathroom where she could hold onto the sink. "I'm enjoying the decorations, so it was worth it to me."

"Yeah, and Zach's sister and her crew will be staying in cabin one. Only cabin three is a waste."

"You just never know."

He stepped into the hall. "Holler when you're ready."

"Yes, sir."

He chuckled and pulled the door shut.

After she'd used the facilities and washed her hands and face, she pulled off her clothes and put the pajamas on. The soft flannel was like being wrapped in a hug. They were a bit big, so she was glad the pants had a drawstring. She tied the shirt up under her breasts to keep the bagginess under control, and leaving a bit of tummy showing.

Brenda opened the door and called out to Thomas. He stopped in the doorway and looked her over, fire lit his eyes and she felt way too warm in the flannel. Then he blinked and cleared his throat and was back to his stoic self. It all happened so fast she wondered if she'd imagined it.

"I can put your clothes in the wash with mine, so they'll

be fresh for tomorrow." He'd changed into pajamas that matched hers. She liked matching, it seemed intimate.

She dragged her mind out of the gutter and muttered, "Um, okay." She felt weird about him washing her clothes but would rather have clean ones in the morning.

"Just leave them on the floor and I'll grab them in a few minutes." She nodded and dropped them, then she was swept up in his arms, he smelled so good, like horse and man, with a hint of sweat. He was strong, she liked the feel of his hard muscles holding her next to his chest. She would be happy to stay in those arms, but he took her to the kitchen table, where the chessboard sat. He positioned her so he could prop her foot up, but she could still reach the game.

"I'll be right back. Go ahead and choose a color and set your pieces up."

Brenda watched him as he strode off. He was a fine-looking man with a strong even gait. She could watch him all day. Instead, she took hold of the white chess pieces and started lining them up on her side of the board.

The wind howled and she hoped they wouldn't lose power; she didn't like sitting in the dark.

∼

THOMAS CAREFULLY GATHERED UP HIS AND BRENDA'S clothes and put them in the washer. He hoped nothing in there was delicate, because he wasn't going to sort them. They had both worn heavy sweatshirts and jeans, so he thought they would be okay. Handling her clothing still caused him to think about her wearing them, and taking them off, so he needed to keep his interaction with them to a minimum, before he did something crazy, like sniff them.

The flannel pajamas had already done a job on him, with

the shirt tied up under her tits and the legs rolled up so her ankles showed. The pjs looked a little big on her, so he wondered if that's why she'd done it. Or whether she was trying to drive him crazy.

If it was the later, she was doing a damn fine job of it. He wanted to grab her and carry her into the nearest bedroom. Then he'd noticed the swelling on her ankle, which had cooled his ardor, as his protective mode kicked in. Immediately he'd gathered her up, to get the ankle back propped up and iced.

Once that was done, his mind had gone back to the bedroom and how if she was flat on her back under him her leg would be good, he pushed those thoughts away and tried not to think about it. Maybe he should search around and see if he could find some crutches for her. It would help to keep his hands off all that warm soft skin. He didn't think they had any out here, but it was a possibility.

Someone could have gotten hurt, and used them, or left them, or maybe they'd had enough up at the house that they had taken the extras to the cabins. Hopefully by tomorrow she'd be able to hobble around a little bit. He didn't know how bad of a sprain it was. Since it wasn't bruising and she'd been able to hobble around on it in the bathroom, he thought it was probably minor, which meant the ice and elevation would work.

He didn't hurry back to the kitchen, but took his time, poking around in closets looking for crutches or even a cane. He wasn't sure how well he would do sitting across from her while they played chess. He would probably play like shit because he'd be thinking about her. Damn.

Back in the kitchen with no crutches or cane he saw that she'd picked the white chess pieces. "Do you want the brownies now?"

"Sure, I'm not going to turn down brownies. Are they cool enough?"

"Oh, they might still be a little gooey. But we can still eat them. Do you want butter or anything to go on them?"

"No, just the chocolate."

He cut the brownies up into nine large pieces. Put two of the pieces on plates and took them back to the table. He liked butter on his, especially when it was a little warm, so he brought the butter and a knife with him.

When he sat down across from Brenda, he concentrated on lining up his pieces. He needed to keep his eyes on the game. She took a bite of the brownie and moaned. Fuck, now she was making sex noises. He tried to turn off his hearing and concentrate on the chess board, but it just wasn't that interesting.

Once he was done with the setup, he slathered butter on the just barely warm brownie. "I like mine with butter."

"I see that." The wind howled, and she flinched. "Are we going to lose power?"

"No, can't happen. We're on solar power."

"Really?"

Thomas swallowed another bite of brownie. "Yep. The whole ranch is on solar power. We get three hundred and fifty days of sunshine, might as well take advantage of it."

"But isn't it expensive to convert?"

"Yeah, there was a chunk of change that was spent, but they figure they'll make up for it not having to run power out this far. And the many times that we did lose power and had to use generators to keep everything moving, with gas prices as they were it wasn't cheap. To keep the horses warm, people warm, water flowing, it just made sense to convert."

He chuckled. "It took Adam some time to convince his

parents and Grandpa K, but he did it. So now the whole ranch is on solar power."

Brenda's eyes had gone unfocused. "Even down in town almost every day has sunshine."

"Up here it's even more so. We don't have as much atmosphere, no smog, just bright sunshine."

"Solar power. Hmm, not at all what I expected. So, what's the little potbellied stove for?" she said pointing at the wood burning stove he'd lit when they first came in.

"It heats up the place up faster than electric heat, but it's mostly left over from the days when we didn't have solar power. They had the electricity running out this far, but the wind and snow and everything knocked it out way too often. And the little stove was the only thing left to cook on."

"So, the barn is temperature controlled, too?"

"Yep. We've got the power, might as well keep it warm for the horses. It's not hot out there, but it's not freezing either. And it keeps the water running."

"That's very interesting. Are there other ranches doing the same thing?"

Thomas shrugged. "I know Adam has talked about it a couple of times at the meetings that he goes to for all the cattle ranches around here. I don't know if he's convinced anyone yet. But I'm sure glad that we have nothing to worry about."

"Yeah, that's great, I don't really like sitting in the dark. I'm not exactly afraid of it, but it makes me uncomfortable".

"I'd keep you safe." He thought about sitting in the dark on the couch next to her, holding her close and thought that was a really fine idea, but not if it would make her uncomfortable. Maybe if they plugged in the Christmas tree. Between the fireplace and the glow of the Christmas lights it would be.... He put a screeching halt to those thoughts.

He needed to keep his mind on track and away from taking advantage of the beautiful young woman sitting across the table from him... eating bites of brownie and moaning. Maybe making brownies wasn't such a hot idea in the first place. But it was too late now, he would just have to suck it up and behave like a gentleman.

"Ready to start playing?" He asked her, when most of her brownie was gone.

She popped the last bite into her mouth and nodded. They'd only been playing ten minutes when he realized she didn't have a clue how to play chess. She seemed to know how the pieces moved, but she had no strategy whatsoever.

"Um, Brenda?"

"Yes?"

"Have you played chess before?"

She seemed to wilt before his very eyes. "Just a couple of times. I never had anyone to practice with. Why, am I playing badly?"

He didn't want to hurt her feelings, so he tempered his response. "Well, not badly, exactly, it's just that, you're going to lose."

"Oh. Well, I know how the pieces are supposed to move. But I guess the strategy is kind of over my head."

"I doubt it's over your head. You're too smart to not be able to understand it. But if you've never been shown the strategy. That's a completely different subject."

"Can you teach me?" She asked sheepishly.

"I can teach you what I know, I'm not the world's best chess player. But I am better than you are."

She huffed. "Well fine, be that way." She crossed her arms over her chest and sat there pouting. Shit now he'd done it. Before the thought was out of his head, she grinned at him.

"Did I insult you?"

Her smile grew. "No, not at all. I was just teasing."

He chuckled with relief. "Now put your pieces back and let's start over."

She whined, "But moving the pawns out of the way is boring."

"You're not moving the pawns out of the way you want to use the pawns strategically."

"It doesn't seem that way to me, just seems like getting them out of the way so the real pieces can move."

"I've seen a pawn win the game."

"Really?" her tone of voice suggested she didn't believe him.

"Yep, they're sneaky. Sitting there looking all innocent and then wham, they take out your queen."

They spent the next two hours playing chess, with him explaining the strategy and how to look ahead a few moves to plan her strikes. She caught on quickly. And the last game they played, he had to keep his wits about him.

When he did barely beat her, she yawned, and he decided to call it a night. "I think that's enough for tonight."

She nodded and then yawned again. "I think you're right, I'm ready for bed. If you don't mind giving me a lift."

"Your wish is my command." They quickly put the pieces back in their container and set it on top of the chessboard which they pushed to the end of the table.

"Providing we can get out of here tomorrow, we'll put that away before we go."

"Do you think we'll be stranded more than one day?" she asked quietly.

"We'll have to see what the snow is doing; the wind didn't sound very promising. Although it could be blowing the storm away, as opposed to bringing more in. It's hard to say, we won't know until morning. Do you want a water bottle for your room for the night?"

"That would be nice. I don't usually get up in the night, so you don't need to worry about me. I'll just use the facilities before we go to bed. And then I'll be good until morning."

"Good to know. I'll leave my door open. So, if you do need me, just yell. I'll hear you. I'm a light sleeper."

He got the cabin ready for the night while she used the facilities. When she was finished in the bathroom, she called out to him. He carried her to her room and set her down on the turned down bed. "There you go. I put a pillow under the blanket for you to put your foot on. If it starts hurting and you need ice, just yell. Otherwise, I'll see you in the morning."

"Thomas."

"Yeah?" He turned back.

"Thanks."

"You're welcome, but it wasn't a big deal. Just Colorado hospitality."

Her smile was slow and a little shy. He wanted to stride back across the room and kiss her senseless. Instead, he turned and walked away from temptation.

CHAPTER 6

*B*renda was tired, but she couldn't help but think back over the evening. It had been so nice just to be normal. She'd had so little of that in her life. Before she'd turned eighteen, she'd had every moment scripted for her by her parents, her nannies, and boarding school. There had been dance lessons, piano lessons, art lessons, conversation lessons, current event lessons; every minute, every hour, every day she was kept busy. When she did have a few minutes to herself, she'd had no one else to play with, or to just sit and talk to.

Until the day she turned eighteen and she had informed her parents she was going to the mineral engineering school in Colorado. They'd been appalled. They wanted her to be a doctor or a lawyer or something professional, but she'd picked a rowdy engineering school. Her parents still didn't know why she had picked that college to attend.

The reason she'd picked it was kind of ridiculous. She'd been at a fundraiser and she'd only been nine years old, but they'd expected her to sit and look pretty. And not fidget. She'd done that, hour after hour. Until she couldn't stand it anymore. Brenda had told her mother she was going to the bathroom. But instead of going to the bathroom, she'd snuck out onto the patio they'd had behind the building.

She could still, to this day, remember how the sun had warmed her skin and she'd felt like she could breathe again. Then she'd seen a boy, several years older than her. He was down in the flower gardens. So, she'd snuck down to see what he was doing. He had some kind of a little magnifying glass, and he was looking at the rocks.

"What are you doing?" she asked.

"Examining these rocks."

"Why?"

"I'm trying to determine what they're made of," the boy said.

"Aren't they made of rock?"

He laughed, it hadn't been a derisive sound, but one of pure joy. "Of course, they're made of rock, but there's different kinds of rocks, you know."

"There are?"

He nodded sagely. "Yes, there are sedimentary rocks, metamorphic rocks, and igneous rocks."

"What's the difference?"

"Sedimentary rocks are made from little pieces of rock, settling, year after year after year, until it squishes together and forms a rock." He pointed to one pile of rocks that had some of the red stones she'd seen in planters.

"Little pieces, like sand from a beach?"

"Yes, exactly. Very good. Often sedimentary rocks are made from a beach or lake, or wind, or, well, a few other things. My name is Clark Madden, what's yours?"

"I'm Brenda Stratton. Nice to meet you. What's the meta, meta…"

"Nice to meet you, too. Metamorphic rocks are those that

have heat and pressure applied to them deep under the surface, they get twisted and hardened by that pressure and heat. Then they get pushed to the surface." Clark pointed to a pile that had some pretty white rocks in it.

"Hmm. What about the ignish rocks?"

He corrected, "It's igneous, those are volcanic."

"Oh, so volcanoes make those?"

"Yes, they do, or lava, either underneath the earth's surface or from a volcano that spits it out."

"We went to Hawaii once."

"Then you've seen lots of igneous rocks."

She didn't mention that she'd seen it from the car window. Her parents had taken her with them, only for her to be shut away in a hotel room with her nanny the whole time. They'd been high up in the hotel, so she had only seen the ocean from the balcony.

"Is that a little magnifying glass?"

"Yes, it's called a hand lens by geologists. I'm going to be one when I get older. A geologist, not a hand lens." He laughed at his own joke.

She looked longingly at the hand lens but didn't dare ask to look through it.

He must have noticed because he asked her, "Would you like to use the hand lens to look at the rocks I've identified?"

"Oh, yes. Thank you so much for letting me."

"Start with this quartz, it's the best of the whole lot."

He handed her one of the white rocks and helped her to see through the hand lens. It wasn't very easy to get it in focus, but he was very patient with her. "Oh, it's so pretty, there are lines in it that kind of shine."

"Yeah."

"What a fun job you will have, getting to look at rocks all day."

He chuckled. "It will be, but first I have to go to school, and it's a very hard school."

"But you'll be a rock expert when you finish?" Brenda asked in awe.

"Yes, I'm going to study geology at a school in Colorado," Clark said.

"That sounds like so much more fun than what I'm learning."

He shrugged. "Yeah, elementary school and high school are not too fun. Regular learning can be boring, it's not nearly as much fun as when you get to select what you want to learn."

"Hmm. That's true. If I got to pick which classes I want to take it would be much better than being told what I have to take."

"Absolutely. But the idea is that you learn the fundamentals that can be used for your whole life."

Brenda wasn't sure everything she was learning would be valuable for her whole life, but she didn't argue. "When did you decide you wanted to be a geologist?"

"Someone came to our class in middle school. He was a geologist, and he told us all about it. From that day forward, I wanted to go to his college. I'm going to, but I have to work really, really, hard and get really good grades, they only take the top ten percent of students in the country. And even after you get there, it's a really hard school."

She didn't know what ten percent meant, but she supposed it was something special. "I get good grades."

"Well, keep it up. Maybe you'll get to go to your choice of colleges."

"I will. Although, I think my mommy and daddy want me to go to Harvard. That's where they went. That's where they met."

"Well, that's a good school, too."

"Yeah, but I don't really want to be a doctor or a lawyer. I think being a geologist would be much more fun."

"I agree with you there, kid."

"Thanks for showing me the rock, I have to get back or my mom will be angry with me." She whispered, "I told her I was going to the bathroom."

"Yeah, I probably should be getting back too, I've been gone a long time. I'm old enough to be gone for a long time, though. You're still just a kid."

She'd gone back to her seat and could sit still very easily after that, as she thought about all she had learned.

That encounter with that boy so many years ago, had given her the direction she'd needed. To break free and choose something different than her prescribed life. Every chance she got she looked up geology. As she got older, she'd asked her teachers about it. Some of them had known something about it, mostly the science teachers. Some of them had even given her some books to read. Others had told her she was being foolish.

Whenever she had the chance, she'd scoured the shelves at libraries going straight to the 500 shelves instead of fiction. When she'd hit her teen years, she'd asked for a hand lens, her father had chuckled and told her it was called a jeweler's loupe. Then he'd said something to her mother about the apple not falling far from the tree and how Brenda wanted to check the quality of her jewelry. She didn't care what it was called or what they thought she wanted to do with it.

Her parents had been horrified when she'd applied to the engineering school in Colorado. They'd worked hard to try to convince her she wouldn't fit in with all those guys. Women were still a minority by a huge percentage. She'd held her ground, even amidst threats of disinheritance, but she knew she had her grandmother's money set aside for college and living expenses for however many years she wanted to attend.

Of course, when she got to the college, she changed her mind, as many freshmen do after seeing all the school had to offer, and decided to major in mine reclamation instead. She really liked the idea of cleaning up the environment, making it better for the future generations. She still had to take a lot of geology, just like almost everyone at the school did. But she'd also had to take a lot of chemistry. Because a lot of mine reclamation was dealing with left-over chemicals used by previous generations to extract the ore from the rocks that it was found in.

She'd also learned when she got to Colorado, just how many mines there were that needed to be cleaned up, both in Colorado, and around the country and even the world. She'd looked up Clark Madden and had found him in the last year of his doctorate program. She'd thanked him for what he'd done. He'd not remembered the incident until after she'd told him all about it.

The memories made her smile. It wasn't always easy, but she was where she was meant to be and that was very satisfying. She reached over to turn off the lamp on the bedside table, pulled the covers up over her shoulders, and shut her eyes.

Her mind wasn't quite ready for sleep as it tried to decide if she wanted it to be sunny tomorrow, or to still be snowing. She had enjoyed her time with Thomas in the cabin. So, if she was honest with her feelings. She would want to stay and have more time with him, but she also had samples that needed to be tested.

She'd gotten an idea that maybe they were looking in the wrong place. Not knowing if it was a valid conclusion or a gut instinct, she'd followed a quartz formation further north.

As she'd hiked, she'd collected samples and labeled their location. Now she wanted to get them back to the ranch so that Patricia and Steve could test them.

So, she was torn between wanting to stay and wanting to go back. She wasn't here on this ranch to just hang out with the hot cowboy, she was here to do a job. So, she supposed she should lean in favor of getting back. Then again, it wasn't up to her anyway, it was up to the weather, or fate, or God, or whoever it was that was in charge of such things. Certainly not her, so she'd see tomorrow about how her day would unfold.

Now she was going to sleep. The ibuprofen she taken while they were playing chess, had worked, and she had a new ice bag on her ankle. It was real ice, so it would melt. Rather than chemicals that stayed cold longer, so she wouldn't have to worry about it getting too cold and removing it.

As soon as her eyes were shut and her brain turned off, she had visions of Thomas floating through her head. The man was pretty to look at, and kind, very kind. He could have teased her about saying she wanted to play chess when she really didn't know what she was doing. Or he could have gotten testy about it. But he hadn't. He'd just settled in to teach her the game.

It was a welcome change from so many others. And it had reminded her of the boy from the party so many years ago, who had explained to her all about rocks, and had changed the course of her life.

Brenda wasn't going to become any kind of expert chess player, but the kindness of the man would remain with her all of her life.

~

Thomas left his door open as promised. He'd pulled off the pajama shirt that matched the pajamas Brenda was wearing. He found that kind of amusing, matchy-matchy.

He turned off the lights, got in his bed, and laid back with his hands crossed behind his head, to think about the evening. It had been pleasant. He hadn't had such an enjoyable evening with a female in, well, maybe ever. Once he'd reigned in the lust — not that it truly had ever gone away — but he gotten it under control, at least somewhat.

She'd said she didn't know how to play chess, and he'd settled in to teach her. The evening had been fun. He didn't know very many super smart people that would have admitted that they didn't know something. He'd so often run into those that were very, very smart, like she was, that thought they had to be intelligent in all areas of their life.

Which just wasn't true. People knew what they'd been taught, or even what instinct had shown them, but that didn't mean that they knew everything there was to know on the planet.

He thought back to the doctor that they'd helped a couple of years ago. His son had wandered off, and they couldn't find him. So, the mother had called in for reinforcements. And he'd been one of the people called in by the authorities to help with the tracking. He had a damn fine reputation in Grand County. And the search had been in part of the area he'd grown up in, so very familiar to him.

When they'd gone to where the boy had last been seen, the father had started going off about how he knew his son was in a particular direction. That he didn't need any help, blah, blah, blah. Fortunately, they hadn't churned up that area too badly with searching for the little boy in the first place.

Thomas could see the trail. He walked a few paces in the direction that the man had said his son had gone, and then saw where the little boy had turned around and come back. When Thomas didn't continue in the direction the father insisted his son had gone, the man had gotten angry, calling Thomas a fake. Going on to say he had a PhD and knew more than some ranch hand, blah, blah, blah.

Fortunately, there were enough people searching that Thomas had suggested that one of the crews could go with the father in his direction, and Thomas would take the mother in the direction he was certain the boy had gone. The mother hadn't argued with the father but just nodded and followed Thomas. She was more interested in finding her son, than being right.

The father wanted to find the son, too. But he wasn't willing to listen to what Thomas had to say. So, they'd split up, each taking a radio and a first aid kit, just in case the child was hurt. Once they'd gotten away from the rest of the searchers, Thomas had started moving faster. The little boy needed to be found before it got dark. They had time, but he didn't want to dally. He wanted to find the child before he got hurt or encountered any wildlife.

The mother didn't say anything, just kept pace with him. He spent about thirty minutes following the trail, until they finally found the child who was sitting on a rock, crying. Safe but scared.

The mother rushed over to her child. "Oh baby, I'm so glad we found you."

"Me, too, mommy. I got lost and I couldn't find my way back. You always said if I got lost to just stop where I was and wait. It was really hard to wait because I was scared. But I did what you told me to do."

She hugged her child. "Are you hurt anywhere?"

"No, I didn't get hurt. I just got lost."

She handed her son, a bottle of water and pulled a snack

out of her bag. Thomas radioed to the other team, and to the coordinator, that they had found the boy, and would be bringing him back to camp.

Thomas crouched down and asked the boy. "Do you feel like walking back?"

"I want to get back, but I'm kind of tired from all my walking."

"Want to ride on my shoulders?"

His eyes grew wide. "Can I?"

"Absolutely. I'll hold on to your feet. If you want to, you can hold on to my head, but not over my eyes or down around my neck or anything like that, just hold on to the top of my head."

"Okay."

After he'd hoisted the boy up on his shoulders, the mother had looked at him like he was a champion. When they got back to the camp, the father hadn't even thanked Thomas. He'd just taken his son by the hand and gone into their camper.

The mother had shaken her head. "I'm so sorry my husband was rude. He's got a bit of an ego and doesn't like being wrong."

Thomas brushed it off. "This was my job, so don't worry about it."

The mother had said, "Well, I appreciate your help. And so does my son. Thanks, and have a good day."

"Have a good rest of your vacation."

"I'll be keeping a closer eye on him."

Thomas laughed. "That's not a bad idea."

Brenda was a lot like that mother had been, humble and grateful. He was glad that Brenda was not so stubborn, or high and mighty as the doctor. She'd thanked him for coming and finding her, making her dinner, and teaching her to play chess. She thanked him all the time. And she was humble enough to say when she didn't know something.

Completely cut from a different cloth than most of the smart people he'd met. He could envision spending many more evenings like that with her. Then taking her to bed and loving her. But that wasn't meant to be.

He didn't know what tomorrow would bring, but he was going to remember today for a long, long, time.

CHAPTER 7

*T*homas was awakened by a gust of wind that rattled his windows. He knew everything was secure. He'd made sure of it last night, both in the barn, and in the house. But as long as he was conscious, he figured he might as well check.

He got up and padded down the hall, in his bare feet, and bare chest. There was a light on in Brenda's room. He could see the light under the door. He thought about stopping and asking her if she was okay, but decided to just keep going, and check the house. When he was assured everything was secure, he went back toward his room.

The light was still on in Brenda's room so he knocked softly, if she was asleep, maybe she wouldn't hear it, but she immediately called out, "Thomas?" her voice sounded a little shaky to him.

"Yes, it's me."

"Come in."

He opened the door and walked in; she was huddled at the top of the bed surrounded by pillows, hugging her knees, with the blankets up to her chin.

"Are you okay?"

"No, I don't like the sound of the wind. Is it going to turn into a tornado?"

He nearly laughed; winter was not a time for tornadoes, but she didn't need flippancy. "No, we don't get tornadoes up here. There's not enough space for them to form with the mountains all around us."

"But this is a pretty big valley."

"Not big enough for a tornado."

"Are you sure?"

"Absolutely. I've lived here my whole life. And we've never even come close to a tornado. The wind blows, there's no question about it, but it doesn't swirl enough, it doesn't form into a pattern that would cause a tornado. It's just blowing wind."

"Oh, Good."

"Do you need another ice pack for your ankle or anything?"

She shook her head. "No, I'm fine."

"Okay, well I'll see you in the morning."

"Thomas."

He turned back at the shudder in her voice. "Yeah?'

"Would you... would you mind sitting with me for a little while." She put one of her fortress pillows up against the headboard.

He ignored the indication she wanted him on the bed and took hold of a chair. "Sure, no problem."

"Could you sit up here on the bed and put your arm around me?"

Dear God, she was gonna kill him. Her in those soft pajamas, next to him in nothing but pajama bottoms, was going to test his control. But he nodded and sat on the bed next to her, and put his arm around her. She cuddled into his chest.

"Thanks, I've never liked strong wind. Even the sound of it is scary. It's probably from the time when I was little, and we got caught in a tornado. I don't know why we were somewhere that had tornadoes. We mostly spent our time in Manhattan. But we were, I don't even know what state it was in, I just remember the sound, and having to sit in a dark room under the ground. I wasn't very old, five or six maybe, but I've never forgotten it."

"You're safe here, darlin'. No tornadoes. The wind blows and it howls, and it sounds like it could do damage, but it doesn't really. These houses were built for this weather. So, you don't need to worry."

They sat in silence, after that, listening to the wind blow. He hoped it wasn't a scary sound for her now. He felt her relaxing. She'd been tense when he'd first sat down. When she started to relax, he thought he should make his escape. He didn't think it was a good idea to hold her all night, things might get out of hand.

Less than five minutes after he'd had that thought, he felt one hand start to move around his waist. He sat perfectly still, barely breathing, and her hand moved to his abs. Soft fingers touched each muscle making it jump.

"Brenda."

"Yeah?"

"What are you doing?"

Her voice was so soft he could barely hear her. "Um, I'm just, you know, touching."

"I don't think that's such a good idea."

"It feels good."

"Yeah, a little too good."

Rather than deterring her, the hand exploring firmed. "We're both adults."

"Yeah, but I'm a lot older than you are."

"That doesn't matter. We're both over twenty-one."

"Yeah, you just barely."

"No, I'm getting up there, not thirty yet, but I'm getting close."

He chuckled. "Sweetheart, I'm closer to forty than I am thirty."

"Still, that's only ten years," She ran her hand up over his pecs. "I'd be consenting. Are you consenting?"

He groaned; they'd known each other maybe thirty-six hours. "Brenda, it's not a good idea."

"I think it's a wonderful idea. I've enjoyed being with you more than anyone in many years, I think you'd be a fantastic lover."

Oh God, she was going to kill him, he'd do his damnedest to be a good lover. But it didn't change the fact that he was still way too old for her, and she was only here for a few weeks.

It was as if she'd read his mind, when she said, "I'm only going to be here a few weeks. So, this relationship would have a termination date. It's not like you'd be stuck with me forever."

He couldn't think of a better way to be stuck. But he didn't say that. Mostly because all the blood was leaving his brain going straight south. His body was on board with the idea of what she was suggesting. He tried to think of an excuse. "I don't think we have any protection here in the cabin."

"Oh, there's some in the girl box, but I'm on the pill, and I haven't been with anybody in a long time, so no diseases."

God, how could the guys she went to school with, not see what a gorgeous woman she was, and be breaking down her door. She ran her hands up around his neck, leaned up to kiss him on the mouth. She tasted like heaven, and sin, and sexy woman. He wanted to devour her, but he tried one last time to pull away to tell her this wasn't a good idea.

She didn't let go, she clung to him like ivy, and put her mouth back on his, giving him no room to maneuver.

He gave up the fight and cupped her head with his hands, pulled her mouth to his, and ravaged it. She gave a little sigh of pleasure in the back of her throat and drew herself onto his lap. She had to be able to feel his cock hardening, next to her thigh.

Then she reached into his pajama pants and took his cock in hand. He about died; the pleasure was so intense. She ran her hand, up his length, and drew her thumb across the head, making his body tingle with pleasure. She wiggled around to straddle him, with a tiny wince for her ankle. But she didn't waste any time unbuttoning her shirt and tossing it to the floor.

He wanted to grab her ass but held back. Her soft breasts caressed his chest, making his temperature rise. She took his hands and brought them up to her breasts, giving herself a squeeze using his hands. It was so sexy; he pinched her nipples and she moaned.

"Now stop hesitating and love me."

He gave up being the gentleman, his restraint was shattered. And he did as he was told, letting his hands roam over her entire body. Her skin was so soft, and he hoped his rough calluses weren't scratching her.

They both still had their pajama pants on, but they weren't much of a deterrent. He squeezed her ass and she arched into him, rubbing her belly across his cock, the soft flannel caressed him as she moved.

Then she was gone. She had leaped out of bed, somehow managing to land on one foot and pushed her pants to the floor until she was completely naked. Her beautiful body on full display. His mouth watered; he wanted a taste of her.

She started tugging at his pants, and he chuckled. "Impatient, much?"

"Yes, very much. Now get undressed, mister. I want to have my way with you."

"I don't appear to have any choice in this matter."

Her hands stilled and she frowned. "If you absolutely didn't want to, and your body wasn't responding to mine. I wouldn't push it. But I think you've wanted me as long as I've wanted you."

She was right, he did want her, so he teased. "How long has that been?"

"Since the moment I drove into the driveway. You went over to talk to Steve, and I couldn't believe how hot you were."

He grinned and rubbed his jaw. "I have to admit, when you got out of the car and stretched, I about lost my mind."

"Well, I hadn't been doing it for that purpose, but I'll take the results. Now, enough talking. Let's get to the doing part."

"Yes, Ma'am." He pulled his pajama pants down and tossed them over the side of the bed. She climbed back up on top of him and ran her warm, wet womanhood along his cock. Then she raised up and started pulling him into her body, slowly lowering down on him, and his eyes crossed in pleasure.

He choked out. "Are you sure about this? One hundred percent sure? Even without protection?"

"I don't have any diseases, do you?"

"I haven't been with a woman in a while. A long while. Out here on the ranch, we work long hours and have little time for socializing."

"Good, because I am going to rock your world, cowboy."

And she did.

~

Brenda didn't know whether what she was doing was ethical or not. But she'd wanted a night with this man. She'd wanted it earlier, but when he'd been so sweet and taught her how to play chess, she hadn't pushed it. Then he'd come to check on her when the storm had frightened her and woken her. She wasn't about to let the opportunity pass.

At least not after he'd climbed up on the bed with her and helped her to relax and not be scared. They'd probably end up going back to the ranch tomorrow. Then there would be no time for the two of them. He'd be in the bunkhouse, and she'd be in the ranch house. She didn't think he was going to want to sneak in to join her in her bed, any more than she was wanting to sneak into the bunk house, to be with him. So, this was probably their only chance.

And she just knew he would be a good lover. She'd been with a couple of guys in college, but they weren't innately kind. They weren't mean, but it was a hard school. So, while they might come together for some mutual stress relief, relationships were hard. Too much focus had to be on school, there really wasn't a choice to be made.

So, while she dated a little bit here and there. It was nothing significant.

She knew this with Thomas wasn't going to go anywhere, because she'd be going back to school in three weeks. She wanted one time with a man who was focused on her. Not on school, not on grades. Just on her.

So, she did initiate it. She figured he wouldn't start anything, because of their age difference. But that was part of what was so appealing to her. Not that he was older, necessarily, but that he was set. He wasn't trying to find his way, he was settled, the guys at school were still trying to figure out who they were. They were still trying to decide who they were going to be, what they were going to do.

They'd gone to school to learn a specific career, so some of them knew where they were headed, but only in a vague way. They didn't know where they would be hired, where they would live, or what their jobs would ultimately be. So, everyone had uncertainty in their future. And when you had uncertainty in your future, certainty in your relationships had to take a backseat.

Not that this with Thomas was necessarily going to be the front seat, either, but he didn't have the uncertainty. He knew where he fit. He knew what his job was. He knew what he was good at and what he was an expert in. He was kind. He was gentle, and at the same time he was assured and strong. She wanted a part of that, even if it was only for one night. Even if it was only for a few hours.

She wanted a part of that certainty, a part of that knowledge of where she might fit, she still didn't know where she would end up. But the idea of being with someone that did know, was very appealing. So, she'd acted on what she was certain was mutual attraction. She'd seen the flare of heat in his eyes a few times when he'd looked at her.

He'd hidden that flare of attraction, of course, as quickly as he could, but she'd seen it. And she wanted to act on it. So, she'd seduced the man, deliberately seduced the man.

His hands were gentle on her skin. But at the same time calloused and rough. He didn't grab, and take, like some younger men did. Thomas pleased her first, slowed her down when she wanted to rush, and gave her his wisdom and strength, and kindness.

That was so arousing. It really didn't take much. She

didn't need a lot of foreplay, who he was, was foreplay for her. When they joined, with her on top, she'd kind of pulled her ankle a little bit.

He'd noticed and shifted their position, so it didn't strain her ankle, he rolled them onto her back, so that she could let her ankle rest. First on the bed, and then wrapped around his waist.

It made her giggle inside to realize that with it wrapped around his waist. It was elevated better than it had been the whole day. But then he'd started moving inside of her. And that was the last silly thought she had.

CHAPTER 8

The next morning Thomas tried to slip out of the bed without waking Brenda, but she was wrapped around him like a python. He was laying on his back with her head on his shoulder and her arms wrapped around him, her legs tangled with his. It was early so she didn't need to wake up yet, but he wanted to check on the horses and the weather.

He thought he could ease away and tried to move one of his legs. She was wrapped around him tightly, so he decided to move, little by little. He'd start with his legs and then work his way up his body until he was free.

He didn't get very far, maybe two inches of one leg, before she said, "What are you doing?"

Not opening her eyes, she wrapped her legs around him more fully, drawing the leg he'd moved back where she wanted it. He lost all the progress that he'd made.

"I'm going to get up and go check on the horses and the snow."

She opened one eye. "But it's still dark."

"Yeah, it's an hour or so before the sun comes up. Go back to sleep."

She pulled him in tighter and ran one of her hands down his torso, making his muscles jump from her light touch. "Since it's still early, we could..." She trailed off. But her hand kept moving lower and lower, until she reached his cock. Which was hardening rapidly.

"We could..." She squeezed him. "...have a little fun first."

She wriggled over on top of him and brought her mouth up to his, to kiss him.

Her smooth soft skin felt so good against his, that he didn't argue. Instead, his hands ran down her back, soft skin beneath his fingers until he cupped her butt and squeezed that perfect ass she had.

She writhed on top of him, her soft breasts pressing into his chest. She kissed him, her hot mouth on his, her tongue seeking. She raised up enough so that he could get his hands on her breasts cupping them. He squeezed them gently and ran his thumbs over her nipples.

With a moan, she reached over to the nightstand for one of the condoms she'd found in the girl box after their first-round last night. She opened it as she scooted back onto his thighs so that she could roll it on him. Then once he was fully sheathed, she slithered back up. Caressing his whole body with hers and took his mouth in another fierce kiss.

Tongues dueling, lips and teeth, crushing and clashing, she nipped his bottom lip, a tiny bite, then licked away the brief pain. With her hands on his pecs, she lowered her body, lining up with his, he felt himself, start to slip inside her.

Brenda whispered, "Yes."

He slid in further and she moaned in what he assumed was satisfaction. She continued her assault on his body. Pleasure streaming through him, as he slid into the warm, yet welcome of her body.

When he was fully seated. She pushed up, arched her back, and he slid in even further. She ran her hands up her body and into her hair. She looked like a goddess in the dark, above him, surrounding him.

He reached up to tease her nipples.

She started moving slightly, just a tiny bit of movement, which was going to drive him completely mad. Circles, grinding her pelvis to his. He let her please herself for as long as he could stand it. He felt her body tense. Tighten on his. She sighed out, his name on her lips, and collapsed on top of him.

He rolled them both over so that she was under him, pulled her knees up, started moving inside her with strong quick strokes. Pleasuring her and himself. When she came a second time, he let himself join her in blessed release.

He quickly rolled the two of them to their side, so he didn't squish her. She was such a tiny little thing. She snuggled into him and he held her, light hands on her skin stroking, soothing. And with a smile on her lips, she drifted back off into sleep. He pulled away and replaced his body with the pillow. She slept on, so he made sure she was covered in the blanket, tucking it around her.

With Brenda back asleep, he stood and stretched, what a great way to start the day. After one last look back at the woman sleeping peacefully, he walked down to his room and pulled on the sweats he'd found, if the snow was deep, he'd come back and get his jeans out of the drier.

He put on the coffee and then pulled the door open. He nearly laughed out loud, the wind had very efficiently blown all the snow into drifts leaving most of the ground bare. Well, no need for jeans yet, he could easily check on the horses in the sweats. He walked out to the barn which had snow piled up in places around it, but the door was clear. Apparently, the wind was efficient *and* wise. He chuckled at his own ridiculous thoughts.

It only took him a few minutes to feed and water the horses, which were no worse for wear from the storm. Then he was back in the kitchen where a drowsy, sexy woman was sucking down coffee, with the cane he'd finally found in the bunk-bed room, leaning against the counter next to her.

"I looked out the window, where did all the snow go?"

"That crazy wind blew it into drifts. So, I imagine the rest of your crew will be here this morning."

"It's still really early though, isn't it? The sun hasn't even been up long."

"Yeah, although the sun comes up later in the winter."

"Oh, yeah, we're only a couple of days from the Winter Solstice."

"Exactly, so if you want a shower before they show up, soon would be good. Our clothes are in the drier. I can make us some breakfast while you shower. I take it your ankle is better."

"It is, a little tender still, so I'm grateful for the cane you found me. I doubt I'll be out hiking around, however. Maybe they can bring the testing equipment with them and I can test samples in here while they continue to verify the contamination field. I think the ravine I found looks promising, but testing will help verify that."

"Yeah, and the fact that the bear was disturbed might be an indication something was going on near his hibernation spot."

"I'll call Steve, after my shower, and see what he wants to do."

She set her coffee cup down, hobbled over to him and kissed him. "I don't know how, or if, we'll be able to be together again, but I want you to know these last twelve hours have meant a lot to me."

He couldn't speak, he didn't know what to say anyway. She patted his chest and hobbled off to the bathroom.

∽

As Brenda limped off to her room to gather up some things out of the girl box, including the sweats, she thought about what she'd said to Thomas. She'd put him on the spot, no question about it, but she didn't really require a reply. She just wanted him to know that he wasn't just an itch to be scratched, that he'd meant something to her.

They both knew it couldn't go anywhere. But she still wanted him to know that he'd been different, that she'd been changed by the experience. He might not realize that, but she did. She knew she'd been changed. And she didn't think she was going to put up with relationships that didn't matter any longer. Scratching an itch was fine and stress relief, too, but it wasn't fulfilling in the long run. It wasn't the same as being tuned into a man, and him tuned into her.

Taking the time to satisfy each other. Not for any gain, just to please your partner. She'd never enjoyed sex like that before. It was a wonderful revelation to have been a part of something so special. She really felt different. She felt different about herself, about her sexuality, about who she was, and where she was going. It was a gift. And she was grateful for it.

Brenda was thankful for the time they'd been able to spend together alone in this cabin. And she knew when she would go forward in her life, that she would look for a man very much like Thomas, that made her feel special. She sighed.

Enough philosophizing, she had to get dressed. Time was marching on ahead of her, and she knew she needed to talk to Steve before they came out, so that they would know to bring her something she could do while sitting on her butt.

In the shower, with the warm water sluicing over her, washing away the evidence of her night with Thomas, it nearly saddened her. But the water couldn't reach her heart, there, the memories stayed safely guarded. For whenever she needed to pull them out and look at them again.

When she was finished, she got dressed in the sweats. She'd have to go find her clothes. but she could wear sweats for a while. She dried off her hair and combed it out, letting it hang damp down her back. She might not be the sexiest thing on the planet, but she didn't feel like she needed to be for him. He accepted her.

She'd like to dress up and rock his world. Maybe for Christmas. She'd get all dolled-up with makeup, jewelry, killer heels, the whole nine yards. But today, she was bare faced, wet haired, and in sweats that were a little too long for her, but she knew he'd like her, just the way she was.

She called Steve and told him about her ankle and that it was feeling better, but she wasn't going to be able to hike around on it. So, if they wanted to bring the test equipment, she could stay at the cabin and do that. She also told him about the formation she'd found and followed, and the samples she'd taken further north.

Steve said, "Excellent. The samples we tested last night, haven't revealed much. I hope you found the right place. Or something at least closer."

"I'm eager to test them."

He said, "We'll be there in about an hour and a half."

"Goody. I'll be ready."

Brenda took her phone back to the kitchen, where

Thomas had prepared an elaborate breakfast for the two of them. The table was covered with dish after dish.

She laughed. "There's just two of us. What's with all this food?"

He shrugged and looked a little sheepish. "I didn't know what you liked, so I made a little bit of everything."

She grinned at him. "A bowl of cereal would have been fine."

He shook his head. "Not on my watch. Sit down and I'll bring you some coffee."

Brenda didn't even know where to start, there was so much food, but she loaded up her plate, realizing she was hungry. Thomas brought her over a new cup of coffee. They started eating in companionable silence.

She said, "Steve and the rest will be here in about an hour. They're going to bring the testing equipment so that I can test samples. Steve said what they looked at last night didn't show them anything interesting. So, he's happy to hear that I found something different."

Thomas nodded. "Good to know. Maybe you hunting further up was a good thing, even if you did hurt your ankle."

Her fork stopped in midair, and she looked at him. "I already know it was a good thing. A good thing for me."

He set his coffee cup down and took her hand. "It was good for me too, Brenda. It was a night I'll never forget."

She felt her heart soar at those words, and gave him a radiant smile, before she went back to eating her breakfast, thrilled by what he'd said, but a little shy at the same time.

CHAPTER 9

Brenda finished putting back on her own clothes and Thomas was gathering up the pajamas, sweats, sheets, and towels they'd used, to wash them. They'd be going back to the main house tonight, so he was getting the cabin ready for the next time it was needed.

"We always leave it clean and ready, we'll be using the main area for the next few weeks, but probably not the bedrooms."

She would have been happy to use the bedrooms a few more times, but had to admit it probably wouldn't happen, since anyone could walk in at any time. Just then Brenda heard a car pull up and one door slam. Their time of solitude was over.

Tracy rushed in and hugged her. "Are you okay? How's your ankle? Are you sure it's just sprained? Shouldn't you go to the doctor?"

Brenda laughed and hugged her friend back. "It will be fine, it's already better today and can bear weight, even if that does hurt some. Thomas found me a cane to use. If it was broken, cracked, or even a more severe sprain I wouldn't be walking around on it."

Tracy pulled back and looked her firmly in the eye. "Are you certain? I know how you like to downplay any issues that make you the focus."

Brenda sighed; best friends just knew too damn much. "Yes, mom, I promise."

Once everyone had checked on her and they had set up the test environment, the rest of them left to go out in the field, leaving Brenda to start testing the samples she'd taken yesterday. One by one she went through the samples. For the most part the concentration of cyanide increased the farther north she had gone. Sometimes there were anomalies but that was not an uncommon occurrence, anything could change how much the plants and soil received the contaminant, a boulder being in the way could cause the water runoff to detour around an area, allowing rainwater to nourish the plants, for example.

Once she was finished, she saw a clear pattern, they would need to proceed further north and east to find and map the full contamination area, but the source was looking like it was due west from where she'd seen the bear.

While she waited for more samples, she thought about ways to keep engaging with Thomas. She was certain, he planned to go directly to the bunk house and avoid her as much as possible. She wasn't about to put up with that. This might be the only three weeks she would have with the man and she wanted to take full advantage of it. So, a plan of attack was in order.

She thought maybe she could cajole him into continuing to teach her chess strategy.

Thomas spent the rest of the day trying to convince himself that it was over between he and Brenda, that there was going to be no more hanky-panky. There was not going to be a repeat of what had happened in cabin two. She was too smart. She was too rich. She was going back to school. She was too young. His head knew all those things, but his heart didn't want to listen.

Unfortunately, his heart was wrong. Every time he walked in the cabin with new samples for her, his heart leapt. She'd smile sweetly and ask him to do some minor chore for her, like hand her a water bottle, make a new pot of coffee, take a note back for Steve. He couldn't resist her requests, but it prolonged the time with her and made him yearn for more.

He finally decided to send Lloyd back with the samples. So, he didn't have to see her over and over again. But then when he did that, he missed seeing her. He was a mess. It was hard to yearn for, and try to avoid, the same person.

After sending Lloyd only a couple of times, the next samples they had to send back he took them. He just didn't want to miss seeing her. She was only going to be here a short while. So, he decided he would enjoy her while he could, even if it was just looking at her from afar.

When he walked in with the next set of samples, she said in a snippy voice, "Well it's about time you brought me those. Why was Lloyd coming?"

He didn't want to admit the truth, so he made up some BS answer about trying to track. He didn't know whether she believed him or not. Because they weren't quite to the tracking stage yet. They continued to follow the surrounding area, so that they could find out for sure where the full contamination area lay. Even if they needed to move into the National Forest land.

He and Lloyd were just basically following the engineers

around while they collected samples, and then bringing them down for Brenda to test. At first, the concentrations were all fairly similar. So, they kept moving. They needed to get to the place where the concentrations of cyanide were weaker, then they would know the upper and lower boundaries of where the poison had leaked.

Brenda appeared to take him at his word that he was tracking, although she did look a little skeptical. "The last set that Lloyd brought was a little lighter concentration. I'm not sure it's enough to say that was the upper boundary, but it was a little bit lighter."

"Well, this set should either confirm or deny it."

"Yeah, exactly."

He said, "We're about to reach the north boundary of the ranch. But we need to know if it extends beyond the ranch and into the national forest, to let the authorities know. Even if we think we've reached the top. It would be good to check just to make sure."

"I agree."

"That's probably going to be tomorrow's chore, however. It's getting late in the day to work without artificial light."

"Yeah, we don't want anybody else twisting their ankle."

He smiled at her. "No, we don't. One invalid is enough."

She was close enough to whack him on the arm, and she did. "Hey, I'm not an invalid I'm just a little less mobile."

"Is that what we're calling it?"

"Yes, it is. I don't believe in being an invalid."

"A woman after my own heart."

She grinned. "Yeah, I can't imagine you in the role of depending on someone else."

"No, I wouldn't take kindly to it." He thought back to his past and some of the troubles he had in school. He'd vowed to never be weak again. The kids had made fun of him for having the same name as a casino town. Of course, it had started as a mining town.

The name was for a family of Native Americans that had lived there, prior to the white man moving in. When he'd come home upset, his father had suggested that he not mention his Native American heritage. It had diluted, year after year with each man in his family marrying a white woman, to the point that he didn't have any distinguishing features of the Ute Mountain tribe. So, he'd not defended himself, and that had gone against the grain.

He'd vowed that once he was old enough and strong enough, that he would no longer hide his heritage. He'd never had to when he was here on the ranch. His great grandfather had worked for the ranch, and his grandfather, and his father, and now himself. There had never been any trouble on the Rockin' K for him or his family.

"Well, I better get back out there," he said to Brenda.

"If you must."

"The next time we have more samples, it will probably be all of us returning."

"Well in that case, give me a goodbye kiss," Brenda said, "I know it can't go anywhere, but the girl wants a little lip lock when she's been stuck doing the testing, instead of the fun part of exploring."

"Behave." But then gave her a kiss. A soft, gentle kiss. When he drew back, she grabbed his shirt and dragged him back down for a much hotter kiss. When he retreated from that one, his head was spinning, and his heart was pounding.

She smacked her lips. "Much better."

He chuckled and walked out the door.

CHAPTER 10

They pulled into the driveway and parked the car on the side of the barn. Brenda crawled out of the car, and saw Tony running hell bent for leather towards her. She hoped he stopped before he ran her down. She hadn't needed to worry.

He screeched to a halt in front of her. "Miss Brenda, Miss Brenda. Papa said you hurt your foot. Is it okay?"

Brenda's smiled at the little boy. "Yes, it's fine, Tony."

"Are you sure? What's the cane for?"

He was a smart little kid. "Well, it's not fine, but it's better. I twisted it. I didn't break it or anything, just twisted it."

He nodded sagely. "That's good. If you break it, you have to have a cast. I had a friend who had a cast, and he said it was itchy and hot. But we all got to draw on it, so that was fun."

She said, "Yes. I'm glad I don't have to have a cast, too."

"I will hold your hand and help you get to the house."

Thomas came around the vehicle and crouched down to Tony's height. "I'll tell you what Little T. How about you

87

carry Miss Brenda's cane, and I'll carry Miss Brenda into the house, so she doesn't have to walk so far."

"Oh, that's a good idea, then she won't have to hurt her ankle."

"Exactly."

"I'm big enough to carry the cane," Tony said and puffed out his chest.

"Yeah, I'm sure you are, you will have to give it back when we get into the house."

"Okay, she can use it around the house, or Nana found some crutches she could use if she wants."

"We'll see. Whatever she wants to do is fine."

Brenda thought that she preferred Thomas carrying her around to any other solution, but that would look weird. She handed Tony her cane. And Thomas picked her up.

Tony chattered all the way to the house, about what he done in the two days that she'd been gone. She wasn't quite sure exactly what all of it meant, but she did catch that he'd baked cookies, made candy, paper chains, and some ornaments for the tree. Some terms she wasn't familiar with, or maybe he was using them wrong. She wasn't sure which.

When they got into the house, everyone was gathered in the kitchen finishing up dinner preparations. Thomas set her on one of the bar stools. And all the Kiplings gathered around her to see how she was feeling. She reassured each one of them, that she would be fine.

Steve came in and cleared his throat. "I believe we found where the contamination is coming from. Actually, Brenda is the one that found it, before she hurt her ankle. The samplings she got from the area, seem to have the most concentration of cyanide. We'll need another day or two to test the outer limits of the contamination, before we start up the ravine, that she thinks might be the source."

Thomas said, "Brenda saw a bear at that location."

Travis looked up from the vegetables he was chopping for a salad. "A bear? This time of year?" Travis shared a quick look with his father before turning back to Brenda.

Brenda nodded and Thomas said, "We were thinking maybe the mining issues had something to do with the bear being awake now. Maybe his food supply was contaminated, and he didn't have enough to eat. Or, well, I really have no idea at this point. But I'll keep an eye out for bear evidence to see what might have disturbed him from his rest."

Travis nodded. "That's a good idea. We don't really want bears wandering around, hungry, in the middle of the winter."

"Right." Meg agreed. "So, while Brenda was hurting her ankle, she was finding the real area. Why did you start up that way?"

Brenda said, "Well, I noticed a quartz outcropping that was headed a different direction compared to where we were looking. So, I followed it further up north not sure if it was intuition or science."

She shrugged. "It wasn't always visible, so I had to use my rock hammer to remove some of the rock around it. And of course, there were trees and bushes in the way as well, but I managed to find it enough to follow it up farther. Unfortunately, I was so intent on looking at it that I twisted my ankle. And then the bear startled me, and I dropped my phone. The bear sat down to eat some leaves on a bush that was only a few yards away. Hopefully the bush isn't contaminated."

Steve said, "Well it might be, but the contamination might be down toward the roots. It might not have reached all the way to the tips of the bush. Depending on how long the contamination has been going on. Poisoning happens pretty quickly in grasses, but not so much in bushes and trees."

Travis said, "So the cattle are more at risk, than the bear would be, just because of what they eat?"

Steve nodded. "We can all metabolize a certain amount of cyanide. But if the concentration is too high and we get too much of it, then it's deadly."

Grandpa K said, "The sickly cattle we noticed first were calves in their first year. The two-year-olds were getting weaker as well. As soon as we realized something was wrong, we moved the whole herd out of the pasture and sent you the first samples."

"Most of them have recovered, we only lost a couple of calves. Going without that pasture, was a bit of a hardship, but much better than losing the whole herd, or all the calves from this year."

"Well," Steve said, "we'll do our best to get that contained. Did you ask the National Forest people about it? Do they have a mine marked on any maps?"

Travis shook his head. "No, if there's a mine up there it's never been reported."

Grandpa K said, "Most likely somebody found it and did a little bit of digging before they were called off to join the Civil War. Most of the gold rush here in Colorado was affected by that."

Patricia cocked her head. "Oh, I didn't have any idea that Colorado was that involved with the Civil War."

Grandpa K said, "Most of the people here prospecting in Colorado were from other states. So, when the civil war started, their families called them home. And most of them went in a rush, so maybe they didn't seal it up properly. Whoever had been digging probably never came back, and then it became a national forest. So even if they had come back, it would have been forbidden to continue."

Travis shook his head. "It must not be very big, or it's all underground, for it never to have been discovered. The question is, what started the contamination now? What happened, what changed, if that mine's been sitting there not contaminating its surroundings for a hundred and fifty years, why now?"

Steve nodded. "That's the million-dollar question."

Meg said, "Let's sit down to the table and have some dinner, you can talk about it more if you want. Or we could talk about Christmas plans."

Tony clapped his hands. "Christmas plans! Christmas plans! Yay!"

Everyone laughed as they gathered around the table.

∽

THOMAS WAS SEATED NEXT TO BRENDA, HE'D NOT PLANNED to sit next to her, in fact he'd tried to avoid it, but somehow, he'd ended up by her. He'd not even seen how it had happened, one minute he was next to Emma with Tony on her other side and the next minute Brenda was sitting down, and Emma had moved across the table.

He suspected it had something to do with Tony wanting to sit by Brenda. He'd heard tales of Tony wanting to sit by the new women at the table, but Tracy and Patricia were new, too. That didn't matter now, Brenda was by his side and he would have to deal with it, without anyone becoming wise to their change in status.

Brenda was making that very difficult, indeed. At first, he'd thought the brushes of her hand were accidental as they passed the food between them. But it didn't matter how he passed her the plate or bowl, their fingers touched.

When they'd passed the last dish, he breathed a sigh of relief that she would stop touching him, but then she'd moved in her chair, so their thighs were side by side, touching from hip to knee. There was no room for him to maneuver away from her, they'd taken the extra leaves out of the table and it was shrunk down to exactly fit the number of people staying in the house.

He about jumped right out of his skin when the sassy little miss laid her hand on his thigh and squeezed. She was trying to drive him insane, no two ways about it. He casually reached down and took her hand by the wrist and laid it in her own lap.

Then when Tony had captured everyone's attention, he turned his head so that it appeared he was listening to Tony and said in her ear, "You need to stop, this isn't the time or place for those shenanigans."

She muttered so quietly he was certain no one else heard her say, "Spoilsport."

He couldn't help but chuckle at her lightning-fast pout. The woman was a firecracker and very good at teasing him to distraction, in front of the whole family, and his boss. Thank God, Tony had everyone in stitches, and they weren't paying him and Brenda any mind.

He couldn't deny that he was enthralled with the woman.

CHAPTER 11

*Just as they were finishing up dinner, there was a knock on the back door, and then Lily's parents walked in.

Lily's dad, Howard, said, "We made it, a little bit late, but we made it."

Lily jumped up and hugged both her parents. "What happened?"

Howard said, "Well, you know, we were bringing that horse for Zach, to start training over the winter break. We've been working with him a little bit over the last couple of months, while Zach was waiting to see if his other horse was going to recover enough for the second half of the season. So, he's prepared, but needs some hands-on training by the man planning to ride him. Anyway, the problem is, we got the horse in the trailer with a little coaxing, and got maybe twenty miles when the horse started scrambling."

"Oh no," Lily sighed and everyone else in the room nodded with her sentiment. Brenda had no idea what that meant and looked at Thomas.

He said quietly, "The horse kind of runs inside the trailer, and thinks he's going to fall down. They can hurt themselves."

Howard continued, "Yeah, he's not gonna be a trailer horse. Won't do at all for a horse that will be spending half the time or more in a trailer. So, we went back, got another one we've been working with to make into rodeo stock, not necessarily for Zach, but just, you know, to sell. That one loaded in fine, and we brought him."

Lily's mom, Elaine took up the story, "So we had to backtrack a bit, and get the first horse out of the trailer carefully so he didn't kick anyone out of fear, which put us later than we had anticipated."

Meg said, "Did you get some dinner, or do you need some food? We still have plenty."

Elaine shook her head, "No, we grabbed a hamburger in Denver on our way through."

Meg nodded, "Okay. We've got some dessert though."

Howard grinned, "I'll take you up on that."

Zach got up and shook Howard's hand and they exchanged a look that spoke volumes, but Brenda didn't know the language. Then he kissed Elaine on the cheek. "I'm going to go check out the horse and make sure he's settled in."

"Some ranch hands came out and started to do it," Elaine said.

"That's good, but I want to, you know, just check my horse. I need to check on him."

"Yeah, I know all about you cowboys," Elaine laughed. "I was surprised when Howard came into the house and let the guys handle it."

Travis shook hands with Howard and Elaine. "Let me introduce you to our engineers, that are here to help with that water problem I told you about."

When introductions were completed, they all sat down while Meg served them a three-layer chocolate cake she called Mayonnaise Cake.

"Where is the rest of the family, Mom?" Lily asked.

"Your sister and her family are going to stay in Denver tonight. The kids were fussing about riding in the car so much, so they stopped at a hotel and they're going to let the kids swim and play tonight, then they'll be here tomorrow."

Howard continued, "And your brother will be along whenever he gets here, you know him. Only God knows what he stopped to look at along the way."

Lily laughed. "Yeah, well he's a college-aged kid, so they do as they like."

Elaine's eyes sparkled, "Isn't that the truth. It's my fault, I raised you all to be independent."

Her dad chuckled "You sure as hell did, and Lily you're right in that crowd too, a little too independent sometimes."

"Now, Daddy."

Howard tugged a piece of her hair and changed the subject. "So, have you engineers found anything yet?"

Steve nodded, "We think we've got a handle on where it's coming from. Brenda found it with great peril to her life."

Brenda laughed, "He's joking. I twisted my ankle is all."

Thomas said, "Well that and nearly had a close encounter with a bear."

Howard and Elaine jerked in surprise. "A bear? This time of year?"

Steve nodded. "Thomas is going to see if he can track the bear, and find out why it was out and about in December. We're going to be testing the outer limits of that area tomorrow. And then we'll start up the ravine that we think it's coming from, the day after. We need to make sure it's not crossing the northern border into the national forest."

"Good to hear. It'll probably take some time to clean it up, if it is a mine, won't it?" Elaine asked.

"Oh yeah, for sure," Steve said. "Depending on the size of the mine it could be a couple of years. No less than six months and that's if it's really small. We'll have to see if we can use the new microbe technology or if we need a full-sized water treatment plant. The microbes are currently only being used on very small mines."

Brenda knew a full water treatment plant would take years to complete so she hoped it was small. The ranch going without using that field for years might end up being a significant burden on the family.

Lily's mom looked at Tony. "Are you excited for Christmas coming, Tony?"

"Yes, I am. It's coming very soon. I get to have Christmas here. And then, after a couple of days of playing with my new toys. I'm going to go down to see my other grandma in Arizona, and we're gonna have another Christmas."

"Well, that's fun."

"Oh, and I get to see my cousins."

"You'll be able to see Lily's niece and nephew pretty soon as well, they'll be here tomorrow."

"Yay." Tony frowned and asked, "Did I meet them, before?"

"Just at the wedding. Drew and Lily's wedding."

"Oh, I remember, Sandy and Jimmy. I liked when she played restaurant, she had lots of paper foods and we ordered them to eat and gave her pretend money. I never got to cook though, I like cooking, especially cookies."

Everyone laughed at Tony's glee.

Thomas whispered, "He does like making cookies, he makes a god-awful mess when he does, but he's always enthusiastic about helping in the kitchen. No matter what is being fixed, he likes being in the middle of it. I think they're still cleaning up from him helping mash potatoes a few years ago. But cookies are his favorite."

Brenda couldn't help but smile and wonder about having a child like Tony of her own. She'd never really considered it, with her career being her only focus, but the idea was strangely appealing.

∼

THOMAS KNEW HE PROBABLY SHOULD HAVE GONE OUT WITH Zach to check on the new horse, but he was having too much fun with Brenda. She'd stopped touching him so much, which perversely, made him miss the little touches.

They'd started a whispered commentary on what was being said around the table. He'd elaborate on Tony, the Kipling family, and the ranch. While she'd make comments on the engineers. It seemed so intimate and a little sneaky, which heightened the fun.

He was going to be reluctant to go to the bunk house when dinner was finished. Even with all the regular guys there, it would be quiet without Brenda to tease and frustrate him.

Apparently, Brenda had been thinking of the same thing, because when the talk had lagged. And there was a slightly quieter time, she turned to him and said loud enough for everyone else to hear. "So, Thomas, are you going to continue my chess lessons?"

He noticed Tracy exchange a look with Brenda, that looked like, what the fuck? Brenda just turned her head away from her roommate and said sweetly to Travis. "Do you have a chess set here in the house that we can use?"

Travis laughed. "Of course, we do. I've got one in my

office, if you'd like some privacy, or we've got one that you can set up at the kitchen table here."

"If you wouldn't mind, I would really like to be in the office. I'm not very good yet, and so I don't really want an audience. Thomas started teaching me last night. All I knew was how to put the pieces on the board, and kind of the way they could move. He was so kind and, well, he was just really nice to me, teaching me the basic moves, and some of the low-level strategy. I'd really like to continue learning while I'm here. If you don't mind him doing that with me in your office."

Travis said. "Of course not, you're welcome to use my office, and you can use the chess set in there, and Thomas is perfectly welcome to help you with that. All of us play chess, so if you want someone else to help you, that's fine, too."

"Oh no. Thomas knows all about it. And, well, he, he's just really nice to me. I've had other times where someone's tried to teach me something and they were just not very nice about it. They were kind of snotty, if I didn't do very good, but Thomas is not like that at all. He was really, really nice last night." Thomas caught her double meaning and shifted in his seat.

"Well, you guys are welcome to my office and my chess set, feel free. And if you want to leave it in whatever configuration you end up with at night, you can do that too. If it's gonna be a multi-day game. "

Brenda laughed. "Oh, we're not quite there yet. Basically, I get a few moves out, and then I do something wrong and he either beats me, or we start over, so that I can learn a better way to go".

"Well, you guys have a good time. First, I would like to ask Thomas to help get Lily's parents' luggage and stuff up to their room, if you can wait just a few minutes."

Brenda said, "Oh, of course, that would be fine."

Drew shook his head. "No, I'll do that. They are my in-laws and since I have the evening off, I'd be happy to get them settled in."

"Very well," Travis said, "just as long as someone helps them get settled."

Howard looked at Travis. "You know I'm perfectly capable of bringing my own luggage in, right?"

"Oh yes, I'm aware, but that's what the young'uns are for."

Howard laughed. "Yeah, we do for them when they're little and they do for us when we're older."

"Exactly. In fact, let's go on into the family room and we can chat while the kids clean up the kitchen and our dishes, and bring the luggage in, and do all the chores that need to be done tonight. We'll take the evening off, the four of us, well the five of us, if you want to join us, Dad."

Grandpa K shook his head. "While I appreciate the offer, Travis, I think I'm gonna go to my own room. There's been a lot of people here today. I'm just going to go put my feet up."

Everyone got up from the table and Brenda took Thomas's hand. "Let's go play chess."

Thomas said, "You don't even know where you're going."

"Yes, but you do."

"Okay, come with me."

When they got to the office. He flipped on the light. Brenda hurried in and quickly shut the door and locked it, then she grabbed him and kissed him like there was no tomorrow.

He wasn't quite sure what to do about that. "Brenda, we're in here to play chess."

"Well yes, but we can kiss first."

He could get on board with that. But he really didn't want

to have anyone come to the door and find it locked. "Just a couple more, then we need to unlock the door."

"Spoilsport."

"We're not having sex in the boss's office."

"Are you sure, absolutely sure?"

He chuckled. "Yes."

"Well, if I only get a couple more kisses." She grabbed him by his ears and pulled his face down to hers, where she put her mouth on his and gave him the wildest kiss he'd ever had.

When they finally came up for air, she panted out. "That's one."

He couldn't believe the audacity of the woman. But at the same time, he enjoyed it very much.

CHAPTER 12

The next two days were pretty much the same as the previous one. Brenda stayed in the cabin testing the samples that Thomas brought back to her. She stole kisses from him as often as she could. Thomas tried to track the bear, both coming and going, but the snow and wind had obliterated the trail.

It took two days to fully map out the contamination section. Steve had insisted on the extra day to be sure that they'd found the full area. Fortunately, it hadn't gone too much farther north than the ranch border. The contamination had run a little bit farther east than they had thought.

They had the space drawn out on the map, which they could give to Travis, so that he could decide how he wanted to handle it. Now the critical issue was finding the reason for the contamination while everything was still frozen.

In the evenings around the dinner table, Tony excitedly told them of all his activities for the day. The first day he'd spent with Alyssa at her house, with Beau coming in when he had the time, they'd made sugar cookies.

Tony said, "All the cookies were round. I made a wreath

and Christmas ball, like for the tree, and a basketball, and lots of other balls. I made a fat Santa face. And I took three round cookies and made them into a snowman. It was very much fun. We used frosting and sprinkles and I had to try really hard not to lick the knife that I was using for the frosting. But I sometimes did lick it and then Aunty Alyssa had to get a new one."

Alyssa nodded. "Yeah, we had to get out more than one knife."

Tony said, "But Emily was even worse. She didn't even get a knife and she kept licking the spoon. Aunt Alyssa got Emily her very own bowl of frosting to put on the cookies. And she still kept licking the spoon. Aunt Alyssa tried to give her a new spoon, but it didn't help, she just kept licking. And then she took one of the cookies she made, and licked all the frosting off, and then put on more. Aunt Alyssa Put that cookie to the side."

Emily said, "Cookies are fun and yummy. Mine were pretty."

Beau winked at Alyssa. "A little bit of a sugar rush?"

"Oh yeah," Alyssa said, and everyone laughed.

Brenda couldn't contain her curiosity. "Why were they all round?"

Alyssa laughed. "When my mom died, and Christmas came, Dad wanted us to be able to decorate cookies like we had done with her. But he didn't know how to make the cookie dough. So, he bought those loaves of cookie dough that you can get at the store and just sliced them off to make round cookies. He bought store bought icing and sprinkles."

Alyssa smiled at the memory and then continued, "When he remarried my teacher Ellen, due to my excellent match making, she got out the cookie cutters, and we started making sugar cookies in multiple shapes, like Christmas trees and

CHRISTMAS AT THE ROCKIN' K

Santa on his sleigh and things like that. But I'd always enjoyed the fun of trying to figure out how to decorate, lots and lots of round cookies. So, I thought Tony might enjoy that as well. And he's got a really good imagination."

Everyone beamed at Tony and Brenda felt a sadness from never having that type of memory, her family had never let her make a mess in the kitchen.

The next night, Tony said, "I went to Aunty Rachel and Uncle Adam's house, and we made white ball cookies, they look like tiny snowballs. We rolled dough into little balls and when they were done cooking and were cool enough, we put them in powdered sugar. Powdered sugar is even messier than flour, Nana."

Meg grinned. "Yes, it is. Did you make a mess with it?"

With a shrug Tony said, "Yeah, it did kind of get everywhere. It was good that the Christmas presents were finished before the powdered sugar."

Rachel said quickly. "Tony, you don't want to say what we made."

"Oh, right. Then no one would be surprised at their Christmas presents." He looked around the table. "Well, you will see them on Christmas. But they were very, very fun to make."

Everyone chuckled at the little boy's enthusiasm for his hand-made gifts.

He said, "And the white cookies are very yummy. Tomorrow, I get to go with Katie. She said we're going to make chocolate cookies."

Katie corrected him, "We're going to make cookies that have chocolate on them."

"Oh. I love chocolate."

"Yes, I'm aware. And we'll have some extra chocolate just for you to munch on."

"Yay. I love to chomp chocolate."

Brenda smiled. She was going to enjoy this Christmas she could just tell. She'd had no idea a month ago when Steve and Patricia had approached them about working over the holidays in the mountains that it would be so enjoyable.

As Tony chattered on, she thought back to that day where they'd been called into Patricia's office.

"You're spending Christmas vacation on a ranch up in the Colorado mountains, and you are inviting us to come along?" Brenda glanced over at her roommate, Tracy, who shrugged.

Patricia said, "Yes, that's exactly it. We need to go up and check out some trouble on a ranch at the foot of the Rocky Mountain National Park."

"It's called the Rockin' K, and they've got some contamination going on. The school has assigned me to this project," Steve said. "Based on the sample they sent us it looks like chemicals from a gold mine."

Brenda knew the most common of those and said, "Cyanide." It wasn't a question; it was the primary biproduct of gold extraction. Her interest was piqued but she didn't know quite what this had to do with her and Tracy, and she wasn't sure she wanted to know.

Patricia took back up the tale. "They're unaware of any gold mines in the area. So, it must be an old abandoned one. They've had to keep their cattle away from the one section, where the contamination took out some calves. Winter snow runoff waters the area. And they're trying to keep that runoff from emptying out into the Colorado River, which runs through their property."

Steve continued, "Fortunately, with it being winter, the stream that forms in the high runoff season has frozen up. So, we'd like to get started on it. Before the spring thaw. They've never had any contamination before, and they've owned the ranch for three generations."

Tracy asked, "So, do we think it's erosion causing it, now?"

Steve shrugged. "That's the most likely scenario, but we won't know for sure until we find the mine. That's where you and Patricia as geologists will use your expertise, to track the beds. Unfortunately, since it's winter we could run into bad weather, so we would need to be prepared for that."

Tracy's eyes sparkled with enthusiasm and Brenda knew the decision had been made by her roommate. She didn't have to go along, but her other choices lacked appeal. Brenda had no interest in tracking down one of her parents. She thought her mom might be in the south of France and her dad in Hawaii, and while the warm weather beckoned, she was not about to play third wheel with her father and his current arm candy, or her mother and her boyfriend, who was only a few years older than Brenda. Nope, not happening. Spending Christmas alone in their little duplex, with Tracy gone, didn't appeal either.

Tracy chirped, "Well, we do usually stay here over winter break. And I wasn't planning to go anywhere this year, and neither was Brenda." She glanced at Brenda who nodded. She knew Tracy had no family to go back to, she and Tracy spent all breaks from school together.

With a little bit of reluctance Brenda said, "It's true I wasn't planning to leave, but the mountains are going to be even colder than down here in the foothills." She always struggled with cold weather. She had a slight build and rarely felt warm.

"True, but it would give you really good experience," Steve pointed out. "If you want to be a mine reclamation engineer, this would be a good trial for those skills. One, or

both of you, might want to use it as a thesis project. It's close enough to drive back and forth."

Brenda thought that was an interesting idea, but didn't really think she wanted to do that. She'd already been working on her thesis project, so taking this on would be a nearly full rewrite. A good one, but not something she wanted to do. But some experience with a real issue would still be good, even if she didn't use it in her thesis. She glanced over at her roommate. "You game?"

Tracy nodded. "Yep. Let's do it."

Brenda sighed. "All right, you've got yourself some cheap labor."

Steve chuckled. "And excellent engineers."

She tuned back into the little boy as he talked about Christmas Eve at church and then the big party in town, with cookies and Santa.

Having Tony around for Christmas put a completely different spin on the holiday. He was so well loved. And so enthusiastic about everything. It was going to be a Christmas like no other. She'd never been around little kids at Christmas. And she had never been allowed to be as enthusiastic as Tony was even as a child. Her parents were very sedate. Tracy had been tossed around from foster family to foster family, so she doubted that she'd had much better experiences.

Some of the foster families had been nice to Tracy, but she'd told Brenda that she never really felt a part of them. Tony, on the other hand, made sure everyone felt included, as did the rest of the Kipling family. Brenda figured the pretty little two-year-old daughter of Alyssa's would be very excited about Christmas as well.

It was a big family, and they were all here. Brenda had to wonder if it was going to feel overwhelming. The tree was practically buried in gifts. Brenda wondered if other guests would also be included, like the other girls' families.

She and Tracy had their own gifts to exchange with each other, and she didn't know whether she should put those under the tree, so they had something to open on Christmas morning, or whether she and Tracy should just open them in their room together, then just enjoy the family opening their gifts. She needed to talk to Tracy about that.

~

As Tony chattered on, Thomas realized he wanted some time away from Brenda. They'd been playing chess every evening after he'd spent the whole day with her, but he wanted to get into town. Maybe buy her some little thing, so she'd have a gift to open.

The ranch hands didn't normally spend Christmas morning with the family. They were always invited to the big brunch on Christmas Day. Most of the time they went, but they never entered in with the other activities. They had their own time in the bunkhouse, playing poker and just taking some downtime. Some liked to read.

It was a good time of year to handle any repair tasks that needed to be done, tack, or boots, or belts, or whatever. There were still chores to be done, animals to be fed, stalls to muck out, and ice to break up in the stock tanks. So, they didn't have a lot of time. But everyone pitched in to get done early, both on Christmas Eve and Christmas Day.

This year, Travis had invited all the ranch hands to join in the activities to help make the engineers feel more comfortable. It would be a large crowd.

Thomas wouldn't mind buying all four of the engineers something, but he needed to be able to get away, to do that.

Katie's store wasn't open late at night. It was open after working hours, but not late, he needed to come up with an excuse to leave early tomorrow, it was only a couple of days before Christmas.

He cleared his throat when Tony paused for a moment. "Travis."

"Yeah, Thomas."

"I need to run into town tomorrow, so I won't be here for dinner."

Travis nodded. "Okay. Just get the engineers back and then you're welcome to go. There's some weather coming in and unless you are planning to use the horses, I want Lloyd to bring them back that evening, just in case we can't get back out there with Christmas Eve coming soon."

Steve said, "We won't be using the horses for another few days and I actually think we could make it back by ourselves. We've been out there a few times now and I think we've got down how to get there and back, if you want to leave a little earlier, Thomas."

Thomas nodded. "That would be great, thanks. Maybe I'll leave about four."

Brenda looked a little pouty at him bugging out on dinner and their chess game, but she would understand later. He had to admit he would miss the kisses she planted on him when they went into Travis's office each evening. He sure wished there was a way to get her alone again.

The next day, Thomas drove into town and went to Katie's general store. She had a little bit of everything in that store, and he was certain he could find some gifts for the engineers. He said hello to the girl behind the counter.

Katie was off today and spending the day with Tony, which was good, because he didn't want her spilling the beans. He walked around looking at everything. He found a small statue made out of coal, a coal miner, and picked that up for Steve. He found a very pretty geode of Amethyst, that had a small silver statue of a deer inside of it and got that for Patricia.

Tracy, hmm, maybe some new earrings for all those piercings in her ears. He went up to the jewelry counter and found some unique ones that were a silver plate with a gold spiral on top of the silver. He thought those looked just like her and were tiny enough they could fit in any set of holes she had running up her ear. So, he picked those up and added them to the stash he had in his basket.

Now the most important one. Brenda. What do you buy a girl who had everything, could afford anything? It took him a long time to decide on what he wanted for her. He searched the whole store.

He thought about jewelry. Women always liked jewelry. He thought about a pretty scarf. Women always liked clothes. He checked out the perfume, and the fancy soaps. Women always like to smell good. He couldn't decide, nothing jumped out at him.

He searched and searched, going back and forth between the jewelry counter, the soaps, and the clothes. He decided to walk around the store one more time and finally, finally found the perfect gift. He chuckled as he paid for his gifts. Brenda was going to get a kick out of what he'd found. It was costing him a pretty penny. But she was worth every cent.

CHAPTER 13

Thomas stopped by the cafe when he was done shopping and was surprised to see Jen there. "Jen, what are you doing here? You don't normally work nights."

"Yeah. But Mary was planning to go tomorrow to her mom's house, in Montrose, for Christmas with her family. But the weather people are saying that the storm that we are expecting is going to start tonight around midnight, with snow, wind, and blizzard conditions. So, I switched with her, she worked my morning shift and I'm working her night shift, so that she could get a head start and get over there before the storm hits.

"Makes sense. Besides that, you live close enough that you could walk if it starts early."

"Yeah, they're not expecting it until midnight though and we don't stay open that long. In fact, you'll probably be one of our last customers."

"Lucky me. I'll have the hot turkey sandwich, that sounds good tonight."

"Got it. Do you want coffee, soda? What do you want to drink?"

"I'll have a coke."

"Cool, be right back."

He sat back and thought about the weather, looked it up on his phone. That nixed the plans for more contamination exploration. He quickly put in a call to Travis. "Hey boss, they're saying that the storm is coming in about midnight, six to twelve inches expected, you might want to tell the engineers they won't be going anywhere tomorrow."

"Yeah, I'll let them know, I was just going to check on that. I had heard it was coming in a little quicker than they were expecting."

Thomas pushed end just as Jen brought over his dinner and a coke. "Don't rush because of the storm, or thinking we want to close. We need to stay open another hour probably."

"Okay, I was going to ask if you wanted to box it up so you could close early."

"No need."

As he ate, he thought about the storm tomorrow, then it would be Christmas Eve, with Christmas following. The three-day break would probably give Brenda's ankle time enough to heal. Maybe she could join in the hunt up the ravine she'd found.

∼

BRENDA WAS BUMMED SHE WOULDN'T GET TO PLAY CHESS with Thomas tonight. It had been another long day of testing for her, the others had focused on the mouth of the ravine and she was bummed she was missing that, too.

She went upstairs to flop on her bed and sulk, but a large box sat in the middle of her bed, she rushed over to it grinning. They had arrived, she'd been worried when she'd heard about the storm coming, but here they were sitting on her bed.

She did a little shimmy, well now she had plenty to occupy herself with.

After dinner she'd get out the list Katie had made her and get busy. Her crappy mood had flown away and she couldn't wait to get started.

Tracy poked her head in right before they needed to go down. "What's that?"

"A secret." Brenda looked around as if someone might be hiding in her room. "For Christmas, if you want to help after dinner that would be fun."

Tracy toed the carpet with one foot. "I would but Lloyd and I kind of made some plans."

"Oh, really. I didn't know you and he were a thing."

"You've been holed up in the office every night 'playing chess'," she said with air quotes. "Besides we aren't exactly a thing, just someone to talk to at the end of the day."

Brenda felt guilty about leaving her BFF every night. "Oh, I'm so sorry. I was so caught up in wanting to kiss Thomas, I left you high and dry. What a rotten friend I am."

Tracy shook her head. "No, we've only got a short time here at the ranch for you to get in as many kisses as you can. We can go back to spending all our nights together when we get back to school. Besides I'm enjoying Lloyd, he's such a sweet guy."

Brenda took her best friend's arm to go down to dinner. She said softly, "No kisses?"

With a sigh Tracy leaned her head on Brenda's shoulder. "No. I need to work on that."

"Just bat those baby blues at him and he'll be a goner."

Tracy laughed as they walked into the kitchen where they found Tony helping 'smash the potatoes'. He looked up and waived with the potato masher, and some potatoes went flying. "Hi Miss Tracy and Miss Brenda, I'm helping with dinner."

Brenda laughed. "And doing a fine job, I'm sure."

Tony grinned and went back to smashing. The girls wandered out into the dining room, where Travis and Steve were talking, with Patricia listening from a chair. Tracy pulled out a chair next to her mentor while Brenda stood close. "What's going on?" she asked.

Patricia said, "Big storm tonight, blizzard conditions, up to a foot of snow, so we'll be staying here tomorrow, through Christmas." She looked at Brenda. "Should give your ankle a nice healing time. Maybe you'll be able to join us when we go back."

"How long is the storm supposed to last?" Tracy asked, while Brenda pulled out her phone to check for herself.

"Travis said probably only a day."

Brenda nodded and turned her phone toward the other two. "That's what the weather app is saying too."

Patricia smiled at her. "Most likely Travis's source of information, too."

Tony led the way out of the kitchen with an enormous bowl of mashed potatoes, the little boy was grinning from ear to ear. "Dinner is ready."

Everyone moved around to their default seats, while the rest of the meal was delivered by Emma, Lily, and Meg. Once everyone had their plates filled, Tony started filling in everyone about his day with Katie.

"We made peanut butter cookies, and each one got a chocolate kiss in the center. We had to unwrap two whole bags of them." He glanced at his mother. "I got to eat the extra ones."

Emma rolled her eyes. "I never would have guessed."

Clearly missing the sarcasm in Emma's tone, he said, "That's why I told you. Then we made cookies that you bake in the oven and put chocolate bars on them when they come out of the oven. I had to be very careful not to touch the pan. When the chocolate got all melty, I got to spread it around with a spatula and then we put peanuts on the top of one pan and pecans on the other."

"I'll bet you licked the spatula when you were done spreading."

"I did, you are so smart, Mommy."

"I am, but the chocolate on your shirt helped me with that."

"Is that why I had to have a bath and change my clothes before dinner?"

"Yes."

Zach said, "You've got a big day planned with Summer tomorrow, but we've got some snow coming in, so it will be too deep to get there in the morning."

Tony tried to be stoic about it, but Brenda could see the disappointment on the child.

Zach continued speaking. "Which is why Cade will be by in a while to pick you up. You're gonna have a sleepover at their house."

"Really? Yay! We're going to make cookies and then go swimming!"

That surprised Brenda and obviously the rest of her crew.

Meg said, "Summer and Cade have a full-sized pool in their house with an exercise room above it. I think they mentioned she and Cade did competitive cheer before she got pregnant."

Brenda nodded and something niggled in her brain as she thought back to the night they had first arrived. "Is she… um…"

Lily said, "Summer was a child star in the TV program *Training up Heather*."

"That's it. I loved the show and I remember her coming forth a couple of years ago to tell why the show really got cancelled. So was Cade the guy she was referring to in the interview?"

Meg smiled, "He was. He was crazy about her and she about him. Hence the pregnancy."

Brenda was in awe that they had a child star in the family, no wonder she had a pool in the house. "Cool, any more celebrities in the family."

Drew grinned at his wife and Lily blushed.

Brenda watched the exchange and started to ask when Lily said, "Fine. I was Ms. Montana a few years ago. The year of the scandal."

Tracy snapped her fingers. "Oh, the year that fertilizer guy tried to wreck the pageant?"

Brenda gasped, "The Baby Pooper guy?"

Drew nodded, "Yep."

Brenda had questions; it had been quite a spectacle for a while with posts going viral. "Oh my God, you all were in the news for a few days. Which one roped him?"

"Cade is the roper in the family, but we all had a hand in bringing him down," Drew said.

Zach frowned and huffed out, "Except for me."

Drew just pointed at him. "Don't start."

"A best friend should be treated as such."

"Stop, you know I thought you were in a rodeo."

Zach folded his arms. "Still."

Emma laid a hand on her husband's arm.

Tony said around a mouthful of potatoes, "Daddy is a rodeo star. Mommy, too!"

Emma asked the little guy, "Tony why are you eating so fast and talking with your mouth full?"

"I have to be done eating when Uncle Cade gets here."

Zach chuckled and Emma said, "Uncle Cade will wait for you to finish your dinner."

"But I have to get clothes and pajamas and my toothbrush and Fred, all packed with my swimsuit, so I have to hurry."

Cade walked in the door and pulled up a chair, he had a plate and flatware in his hands. "No need to rush, big guy. I came by to mooch some dinner. Summer needed a nap."

Meg asked, "Is she okay?"

Cade nodded and glanced at Tony, "Yeah, just tuckered out. If you don't mind, I'll take her a plate."

"Of course."

Brenda wondered if Summer was tired from getting ready for Tony's sleepover. Or if she was resting up for it.

CHAPTER 14

*T*homas was restless, when he'd gotten up this morning and looked out, there had been a ton of snow on the ground, a good three feet, maybe more. But the sky was blue, the storm gone. And there were no more storms projected this weekend.

The snow had started about eleven with big fat flakes drifting down covering the ground, then the storm had kicked in and had howled from midnight until about six this morning. Blowing snow, zero visibility, frigid temperatures.

He'd thought of Brenda when the wind howled and hoped the sound hadn't bothered her. Contemplated going out in the storm to see if she needed him and looked out, but visibility was nil, and she was safe. Also considered texting her, but if she was asleep, he'd make things worse instead of better.

He and the others in the bunk house had looked out about six and then scanned the weather app, which said the snow should stop any time, so they waited a few minutes to start the winter chores. By six-thirty the skies were clear, and they could see the storm moving away from them.

Thomas joined the rest of the hands and family to get the

morning chores done, which consisted of more work than a normal winter day. They'd had to shovel a path from the bunkhouse to the barn. And they'd also done one to the big house, so that everyone could get around to where they needed to go. Later someone would take a tractor outfitted with a blade and clear a path to the other houses, that were set out further.

The ice in the stock tanks had to be broken up, both near the barn and out in the fields. They had to feed the horses. Take hay out to the cattle, and make sure none of them were trapped by the snow. Dig them out if necessary.

If it got warm enough the snow would melt, but he didn't think the frozen ground would soak it up, so it could turn to ice at night when the temperatures dropped. If the ground was warm enough the snow would turn to mud, which was actually harder to maneuver in than the snow or ice. But they had the equipment needed to do the job. They got all the morning chores done and came back for lunch.

Thomas opted to stay back during the afternoon chores, since he and Lloyd were assigned to the engineers today. He didn't know if they would need him, but he hadn't wrapped his gifts yet. When he finished wrapping the restlessness had hit him. He wanted to go up to the big house, to see if he could be useful, which was just an excuse, what he really wanted to see was Brenda, to make sure she was doing okay after the wind. But he didn't really have an excuse to go up.

He couldn't track anything in snow. That and playing gofer was his main job for the project. So, he tried to find something to make himself useful. He wasn't succeeding at that very well when someone knocked on the bunkhouse door. He was surprised, usually nobody knocked.

He got up to answer it, and found Brenda standing there. "What are you doing out here?"

She smiled her killer smile. "I'm coming to find you."

He managed to answer her even though his head was spinning. "Why?"

"Because we've been looking over the maps. And I thought maybe it would be good to have you there, too. So that you could give us any insights that you know."

"But the snow and your ankle."

"I was careful and it's feeling better."

"Did the wind keep you up last night?"

"No, I just remembered what you said and imagined you were holding me so I could sleep."

"Oh, well good. Let me grab my coat."

Brenda's eyes darted around. "Isn't anyone else here?"

"No, they're out with the cattle. Making sure none of them get into trouble. The young ones aren't very stable in this much snow."

"You didn't need to go with them?" she asked.

"No, they can handle it. And I had some other things I needed to do."

"Oh, are you busy, then? Do you have time to come over?"

"Sure, I have time, I've gotten the tasks done, no worries." He grabbed his coat and put it on, then moved to reach for his boots.

She walked into the bunkhouse and shut the door. "Well, if no one else is here, maybe we could…" She didn't finish her sentence. She just grabbed him by his coat lapels and pulled him down for a hot, steamy kiss.

When her mouth left his, she purred, "I missed you last night."

"I think I can tell."

"How soon will everybody be back?" she asked.

"It's hard to say, they could come back any minute."

Brenda pouted, it was very sexy, that little pout, and he actively wished the others wouldn't be back soon.

"Well darn, I thought maybe we could have a little fun, you know, naked and in your bed."

"Probably not a good idea, this time of day."

"Well, shoot." She shrugged. "All right then, let's just go up to the house. Unless we have time for another kiss or two."

He said, "We could have another kiss or two."

"Oh, goody," she said and launched herself at him. He managed to catch her, barely, then she put her hands around his neck and her legs around his waist.

He pushed her up against the wall. And they started kissing like there was no tomorrow. They might have stayed there all day if he hadn't heard some of the men returning.

He pulled his mouth away from her greedy one. "I think they're here. Let's go on up to the house and look at the maps."

With a sigh, she slid down off him. "All right."

Brenda stepped back so he could pull on his boots, hoping his erection would go unnoticed. The door opened and one by one the men came through the door, kicked off their boots and continued into the bunk house.

Brenda chirped to each one, "Hello. I just came to get Thomas; we have some questions."

When she got to Lloyd she said, "You can probably come up to the main house too. You might have some expertise to add as well."

Lloyd said, "I'll do that. Let me wash up first and then I'll come up."

"Okay."

Lloyd grinned at Thomas, as they passed each other.

Thomas knew what Lloyd was thinking. He just shook his head and kept on following the girl.

∼

Brenda was very pleased with herself; she'd gotten some nice kisses out of Thomas. It was just her luck the guys had come back so quickly. She might have convinced him to give her an orgasm or two, if they hadn't been coming back soon.

She couldn't figure out how to get some time with him, away from all the others. There was too much snow to go up to the cabin and Christmas Eve would be here tomorrow. And they would be busy with doing Christmassy things for two days. Tony had gone on and on about all the Christmas activities his family did and insisted that all of them must participate in each one.

When Tony had stopped to take a breath, Brenda had asked, "So Tony, of all those activities that you've been talking about which one's your favorite? Besides Christmas morning, of course and opening all the gifts."

Tony looked at her for a moment. His brows scrunched as he thought. "Christmas Eve, after the party in town. That's my favorite."

"Can you tell me why?"

"We get to open one present. And what's in the present is new pajamas, and a book. Then, after everyone has opened their presents, we all go put on our pajamas and put our book by our bed. And then we all come down to watch a movie. A Christmas movie."

He grinned. "And we have popcorn and hot chocolate and Christmas cookies, while we watch the Christmas movie."

With hardly a breath he continued. "And then we put out milk and cookies for Santa. And then we go to bed and sleep. So that Santa can come, and the night goes faster. And then in the morning, I read my book, while everyone gets the horses fed, the cattle taken care of, and breakfast cooked. Then someone comes to get me, and we get to go down, have breakfast, and open presents.

"But the best part is the movie. In our new pajamas. The whole family, squished together, watching the movie. It will be so much fun to have you there too Miss Brenda and Miss Tracy and Mrs. Patricia and Mr. Steve."

Brenda smiled at the little boy. "That sounds like a lot of fun Tony, we will be happy to watch the Christmas movie with you."

Brenda had noticed a yearning look in Tracy's eyes before she'd looked down at her plate.

Brenda had wished with all her heart that she'd known about the tradition; she would have bought her roomie a new pair of pajamas and a book. Tracy read everything; she wasn't the least bit particular. When Brenda had asked about that, Tracy had just shrugged it off and said books were a great place to go when she was lonely or needed a distraction, and she'd not often had a choice of what to read.

Brenda turned her thoughts back to Thomas, thinking about Tracy's upbringing hurt too much. Lust was an easier subject. She wondered if maybe they could make plans, deliberately, to go up to the cabin for New Year's Eve and New Year's Day. If Thomas could get off the rotation of chores for the day. Then at least she'd have something to be looking forward to, but ten days was a long time to wait.

She slowed down.

"Is your ankle hurting?"

"No, it's fine. I was wondering if just the two of us could maybe spend New Year's Eve in the cabin."

Surprise covered his face. "I, um, don't know. I'd have to ask Travis."

"Will you?"

"Sure. I'll catch him alone and ask."

"Good." She turned to continue to the house.

It took him a moment to get moving, but then he walked with her back to the house, so he could help with the planning for after Christmas. They didn't have long to search for the mine, and she had to hope the weather would hold enough to start moving up the mountain.

They'd set up the maps and a command center in a spare room that seemed to be a catchall, there were craft supplies, toys, games, books, a sewing machine, and a child's toy drum set. Fortunately, everything was moved to the side and there were some folding tables that they had just enough room to set up. One table held the maps, and a second table held their samples and test equipment. They'd finished with the last samples from yesterday this morning and had marked the results on the map.

Steve looked up when Brenda and Thomas walked in the door. He said, "Oh, just the person we wanted to see. Can you come over here and take a look at these maps with us, Thomas?"

Thomas joined them at the map table. "Sure thing."

Steve said, "Thanks for going to get him, Brenda. I didn't even think about your ankle when I sent you to do that. You didn't hurt it, did you?"

Sometimes Steve's head was in the clouds, or if truth be told, his one-track mind was focused only on the task at hand. "No, it's fine," she said, with a secret smile. Knowing that she would happily trade a little pain for kisses any time.

Thomas looked over the work area. "You've got a nice setup going in here."

Patricia said, "Yeah, it's just perfect. Even with all the boxes and toys."

Steve pointed at the map. "So, we were looking at this ravine Brenda found, on the topographic map. It looks like there's a few branches off of it. We were trying to decide whether we should be methodical about it and go up each small branch as we reach it, or whether we should go all the way straight up to the top and work our way down and hit the branches only if we need to."

Thomas looked at where he was pointing. "Well," Thomas said, "it's possible that there might be a small mine on any one of the branches. But an easier area to mine is right here, where there's a little bit of a flat spot, a wider spot. That would make mining easier, I think. But I think Lloyd would know better than I do."

Just then Lloyd walked in the room. Brenda noticed Tracy quickly glance at him with a smile.

"Oh good. Thanks for joining us, Lloyd." Steve said, "So we're looking to start up the ravine, after Christmas, and we're trying to decide if we should go methodically up each one of the branches, or if we should just stick to the large ravine and go straight up."

"The branches are pretty small, pretty narrow. So, I'm not sure why somebody would go up them and try and mine them." Lloyd said, "I would think, going straight up would be the best use of time."

Brenda was standing next to Thomas looking at the map, enjoying the man's warmth and scent. "What if we compromise and do both?"

Patricia looked at her, "What do you have in mind?"

"Well, what if we just go like a couple of yards up each one of the branches, take a few samples, and then continue up the ravine. That way we're not spending a lot of time on the branches. But we could see if the concentration is higher in them than the main ravine."

Thomas looked at her. "That's a good idea."

Steve said, "I agree. I think maybe ten feet would be good, just far enough in, that any contamination wouldn't be from the main ravine."

Lloyd grinned. "That's exactly it. Enough so that we could see if the concentration is less in the branches or more."

Patricia nodded. "Perfect. We'll do that. That won't take a lot of time, since we're not going to the end of each branch, we're just going in a little bit. But we'll know we've been thorough."

Brenda noticed Lloyd carefully studying the map. He pointed to one spot. "This looks a little odd right here. The patterns don't quite match."

They all looked at the spot where he was pointing.

"They don't do they?" Steve pulled out a magnifying glass from his pack. "That might be something worth looking into. It's pretty far up."

"It is, but maybe they didn't come from the ranch area, maybe they came down from the county road. Of course, roads wouldn't have been there a hundred years ago, but there may have been trails. Oftentimes, the county roads are built on trails." Thomas tapped the county road.

"You might be right there." Lloyd said, "look it's not very far away from the road. It's quite a distance from the ranch, but it's not very far from the road."

"Interesting, coming up from the ranch, it's gonna take us a while to get up there unless we go just straight there."

Patricia shook her head. "I don't think that's a very good idea. I think we need to continue taking samples, as we go up farther away from the ranch. because the contamination should increase as we go. And then when it goes away completely, we will know we're above the mine. Then we can search between the high concentration and the no concentration to find the mine."

"Yeah, if we start from the top, we might lose it completely," Steve said.

Thomas said, "I don't think there's any reason to change the strategy now. You guys are the experts. We're just along to help. I want to keep an eye out for anything that indicates where the bear came from as well. That snow is not going to help my job tracking. But there's other places to look, than just on the ground. So, as we move up the ravine, I'll keep an eye on that."

Patricia looked at each of them. "Sounds like we have a plan."

"It does indeed. Well, I think we're done here for today," Steve said. "We've got Christmas Eve and Christmas Day, next. We'll start out the day after."

Brenda was looking forward to traveling up the ravine, now that her ankle was feeling better. She hadn't tested it for hiking, she was just walking around in the house and out in the yard, but she wasn't feeling any pain from it at this point. So, another two days of healing would help, and if she wrapped it and then put on her hiking boots, she thought she'd be fine. She didn't want to be left behind at the cabin while everyone else went out and found the mine.

Thomas said, "Sounds good."

Brenda looked at him pointedly, and said, "You mentioned needing to ask Travis a question."

He frowned at her but didn't argue. "Yes, I do. I'll see you at dinner."

CHAPTER 15

As Thomas left the room, Brenda heard a door slam. Tony was home. They could hear him charge into the house, even before he started calling for his parents.

Brenda smiled at the sound of the little boy coming into the house. She couldn't wait until dinnertime, to hear all about his big adventures. Him spending the night at Summer and Cade's house last night was probably the highlight of his week.

They had a swimming pool after all, and Tony liked nothing better than swimming. At least that's what she'd been told. He seemed to be enjoying his time with all of his aunt's, getting ready for Christmas. He'd made different Christmas cookies at each house that he'd gone to.

The weekend before, when she'd been hurt up at the cabin, he'd helped make several kinds of candy. Fudge, divinity, candied almonds, and peanut brittle, as well as some pressed cookies that he got to decorate with sprinkles. He'd had a very big weekend, with his mom, grandma, and Aunt Lily.

Thomas had clued her in that some of the reason for the

time spent at the different houses was to give Zach and Emma some time off to work with Zach's new horse. To start getting him trained and see what his strengths would be for the various events Zach and Emma participated in. Knowing that made a lot more sense as to why he was going to the different houses.

She wondered what kind of cookies he'd made with Summer. She was certain she'd hear about it soon enough. Dinner was only a few hours away. She heard the little boy charge up the stairs. Apparently, his parents were in their room.

She thought that they had a solid plan for working to find the mine. They only had a couple of weeks left. The plan was to leave on Sunday the ninth of January, School would start on the following Tuesday.

If they took New Year's Eve and New Year's Day off that cut their days down even more. It would be good if they could find the mine, and at least start to determine what kind of reclamation was going to be needed before they had to go back to school.

Brenda realized she was going to miss the ranch when she went back to college, she'd had a good time here. The family was very friendly, and she was going to miss Tony even more, since he was going to leave, just a couple of days after Christmas. He'd be spending his New Year's down in New Mexico, then Zach had to be in Denver by January seventh to join the National Western Stock Show and Rodeo. The little boy had an interesting life and seemed to enjoy every minute of it.

∽

THOMAS LEFT THE ENGINEERS, SHAKING HIS HEAD AS HE went. Brenda was quite the piece of work, nudging him to go see Travis, so he could whisk her away for a night of sex. He couldn't argue that he wouldn't enjoy that because he certainly would. But for her to be so bold in front of all the other engineers, and Lloyd, was certainly different than the way he would have done it.

He went down the stairs and over to the office, where he'd been spending so many nights with the woman playing chess, and exchanging kisses. Fortunately, Travis was alone in the office. So, he knocked on the doorframe.

Travis looked up.

"Do you have a minute?" Thomas asked.

"Sure, come on in."

"Mind if I shut the door?"

Travis's eyebrows rose. "No, go ahead."

Thomas shut the door, went over to the desk.

"Have a seat."

Thomas sat. Not sure that he really wanted to sit. He felt like pacing, but he sat.

"What can I do for you?"

"Well." He took a big deep breath, blew it out. "Brenda would like to spend New Year's Eve at the cabin."

"Oh, that's fine with me. Her and Tracy, or all four of them."

"No. Not exactly, um."

"Spit it out," Travis said.

"She wants her and I to spend New Year's Eve at the cabin, alone."

Travis chuckled. "Ah, I see, the girl's got a crush on you, does she?"

"Yeah, I guess you could call it that. She's only here for a few weeks so…"

"I get it. Nothing serious. But she wants some time alone with you."

"Yeah, she does."

Travis said, "That would be fine. There's no reason why you can't take New Year's Day off to have some time with the lady, but you're also welcome to spend time with her in her room."

Thomas looked up. "What?"

"We've never had rules in the house about consenting adults having sex. Once everyone hit eighteen, we figured they were adults, and they could make their own choices." He sighed. "I'd rather not have had Emma get pregnant so early in her high school years. But you're an adult, Brenda's an adult. If you two want to spend time together, no one's gonna look cross-eyed at you."

"Seriously, you have no qualms about me in Brenda's room at night?"

"Nope, certainly isn't a firing offense, you two are adults. If you want to come spend the night, I have no problem with it."

"And Meg?"

Meg has no problem with it. "Hell, Alyssa moved into Beau's room before Rachel came."

"Well, that's true."

"It didn't take too long before Rachel moved into Adam's room."

Thomas said, "I guess I saw Katie and Summer's vehicles here, a time or two overnight."

"Yes, you did."

"Thanks, I appreciate it. But I still would like to take her up to the cabin over New Year's Eve, give her a little special celebration."

"You do that, make sure you get some flowers and some

champagne, some chocolates. Hmm, maybe I should do the same in Cabin One, one of these days," Travis said rubbing his chin. "There's no reason why you can't give her a little extra attention. And I should do the same with Meg. Women like a little romance now and then."

"I'll do that. Thanks, boss."

Travis just grinned at him. "The college is only two hours away, you know."

Thomas shrugged. "Yeah, it is pretty close. I'm gonna go help with the evening chores. I'll be back for dinner."

"Leave the door open when you go."

Thomas joined the family for dinner, he'd decided not to mention his conversation with Travis until after Christmas, if he could avoid it. The less people in the house, to possibly bump into, when he joined her in her bed the better.

∽

BRENDA WAS SEATED NEXT TO THOMAS, AS CLOSE AS SHE could get. "So Tony, how was your day at Summer and Cade's?"

"Oh, we had so much fun, Miss Brenda," Tony said. "I got to spend the night and we watched a movie and had popcorn. Then in the morning we had breakfast, Aunt Summer made eggs with cheese on top and bacon. After that we started making cookies, we made two kinds of cookies. One is called pizza cookies."

Cade, who was having dinner with them and taking a plate back for Summer, chuckled. "Pizzelles."

"That's it. They're flat cookies and they have a design in them. You kind of make them like waffles, you put them in a thing that looks kind of like a waffle maker."

Brenda nodded. "I know just what you mean, what kind of flavoring did you use?"

"We used two kinds, we used one that tastes like licorice, and one that is peppermint. And we made the peppermint dough a little bit pink so that everyone would know which was which."

"Oh, how fun. Did you say that you make two kinds of cookies?" Brenda asked.

"Yes, we made lace cookies. And those are fun because you put just a little ball of dough on the cookie sheet, and it gets really big and really flat. And if you catch them at just the right temperature you can make them in different shapes. We have flat ones, and we have ones that make a tunnel, and we have some that make a taco. Aunt Summer said that we could fill the ones that looked like a taco, and also the ones that look like a tunnel." Tony's eyes flashed with mischief. "Sometimes they would get too cold and then they would break rather than curl. So, I got to eat those ones."

Brenda glanced at Emma, who was shaking her head. "Another sugar rush, great."

"No, I don't think so, Mommy. Because after we made all those cookies, then we went swimming. And that was very fun, lots of splashing and playing. Uncle Cade is splashy too, but Aunt Summer is the fastest."

Cade ruffled Tony's hair. "That she is. Swims like a fish."

Tony continued his tale. "And then, while Aunt Summer took a little nap, Cade and I went to the gym, and we lifted weights. I'm very strong. I could lift the weights that were two pounds, Cade is stronger, and he lifted bigger ones, but he only let me lift the little ones. I think I could lift heavier ones, but he said not today. It was still fun and I'm very strong."

Emma and Zach both nodded.

Tony wasn't finished. "And we got to run on the running machine. And there's big mirrors in the room, and I made faces in the mirrors and danced around and watched myself, while Uncle Cade laughed. So, I burned off all those sugars in the swimming pool and weight room. Mommy. And I only had two cookies after that. So, I'm fine."

Brenda didn't want to laugh about the fact that a little boy with that much energy, had had cookies, after working out.

Emma looked at Cade. "Your time's coming, brother."

Cade said, "I have no idea what you're talking about."

"I do, I do," said Tony.

"What's that Tony?" Cade asked.

"We have lots of toys, that you bought me, from when I was little all set aside to give to your children."

"What?" he asked. Now Brenda could hear trepidation in his voice.

Tony grabbed his uncle's arm. "Yeah, like the drum set, and the little dog that barked and jumped, and the robot that talked and flashed lights, lots of the things that you bought me. They're all ready to give to your new baby. Well, after it gets a little bit bigger."

Brenda was certain she saw fear in Cade's expression, and his skin had turned pale. "But what if we have a girl?"

Tony laughed. "Girls like to play with dogs and robots and drums too, Uncle Cade.

"I thought the batteries in the dog were dead."

Emma smiled sweetly, "Not to worry brother dear, I sent it to the manufacturer to have them put in a new one, they guaranteed me it would last a minimum of five years."

Cade shook his head. "I think I better go home now. I'm going to take a plate for Summer if you don't mind, mom."

"Not at all. She's feeling okay, isn't she?"

"Oh yeah, just a little worn out. Tony is very enthusiastic about life."

Emma nodded and said, "Yes, he is. He's very fun."

Tony beamed at his mother. "I am. 'Specially when I have cookies and candy."

Brenda could just imagine, and she could tell by Emma's expression that paybacks were going to hit Cade hard. She wondered if his sudden departure was to go and warn Summer.

CHAPTER 16

Christmas Eve day had a lot of activities planned. The Kiplings held a big brunch for their ranch hands after they got all the morning chores done. Even though the next two days were holidays, they still had to get the animals taken care of. There wasn't really a whole true holiday for ranchers, because cattle or the horses or whatever animals happened to be there, couldn't just be ignored for two days. They still had to be fed and taken care of.

Everyone tried to pitch in to help. Brenda even asked if there was something she and Tracy could do. They'd given them a very simple job of putting grain into each animal's feeding trough with very explicit instructions.

She and Tracy were doing that together. Well, not exactly together because Brenda was doing the horses, and Tracy was doing the cattle they had indoors. The main concern was that they couldn't mix the feed for the two or even the scoops that they used.

The food was at two different ends of the barn, the instructions were the same, but they had to be very careful not to get any cattle feed in with the horses. It was dangerous to them. Poisonous actually, which made both Brenda and Tracy a little nervous. But Travis assured them that as long as they did their own side of the barn, everything would be fine, and it would be a big help to allow the others to do chores that were more difficult.

Brenda carefully scooped the correct amount of food into each feeding trough for each horse. Giving any of the horses that came near a soft pat on the nose.

The snow from the day before, had melted during the day and turned to ice at night. She was surprised how fast that had melted with the sunny temperatures of yesterday. The wet didn't absorb into the ground because it was frozen solid, so they had put down some straw to keep it from being too slippery when it froze. Colorado had such funny weather. She'd noticed it down in Grandville where the school was. But up here in the mountains it was even more obvious.

After they had the animals fed, she and Tracy went in to see if they could help get the breakfast set up. It was determined that they could help carry in some of the food. Because there was going to be so many of them, they were using the table as a serving center rather than sitting down at it, everybody would just mill around, and eat the finger foods that had been provided.

She was surprised to see pancakes and French toast fingers, that could be dipped in little containers of syrup, with all kinds of breakfast meats. There were some pancakes, wrapped around sausage links. That could also be dipped into the little pools of syrup. There were all kinds of pastries. Brenda had to wonder if they were handmade or store bought, she thought maybe they were a little bit of both. But she didn't know for sure if someone had gotten out to go into town.

There was plenty of eggs as well. Mini quiches, scrambled eggs, and hard boiled, with hash brown patties. There was a cut up fruit salad that while it couldn't be eaten with their fingers, it was easily eaten standing up out of the little plastic cups. There was lots of coffee, hot chocolate, warm apple cider, and orange juice. She was surprised to see mimosas and Irish coffee.

Some of Tony's cookies had been part of the food on the table. He made sure everyone tried at least one and then pestered them to death about whether they liked it or not, of course no one would ever say they didn't like them. But the truth was, his cookies were very good. His aunts had made sure of that. He beamed with pleasure at each comment.

Everybody started coming in. Singularly or two at a time. And then there was a crowd that came in that had been out taking hay to the cattle out in the field. There was talk, laughter, and a lot of eating. Brenda didn't circulate. She and Tracy stayed in one area. Several people came up to talk to them. As they moved around through the crowd.

She didn't know if Tracy was feeling the same way that she was, she felt a little out of place among this group. Their mentors on the other hand seemed to take it all in stride and were circulating.

There was a lot of joking and teasing. It didn't seem to matter which ones were the bosses or the owners, or which ones were the employees. Everyone was treated the same. Brenda found that refreshing, her family certainly did not treat people like that. They were very class conscious. She'd always been taught that she was a little bit better than everyone else.

She decided she liked the philosophy of the Rockin' K better than her family's philosophy. She vowed when she went out in the world, after graduating, that she would take the Kipling family philosophy with her, instead of her own family's.

She noticed Tony was very good with Alissa's little girl. He was very patient with her and she adored him, it was obvious. They weren't together very often with Tony on the road all the time, so Brenda was kind of surprised by his caring attitude. But it did seem to be a family trait. So maybe he just learned it by watching others.

The brunch lasted several hours before everyone started splitting off. She'd had a wonderful time, probably the best Christmas Eve morning of her life.

~

THOMAS WAS LOOKING FORWARD TO THE CHRISTMAS EVE celebration. He liked going to the church with it all decorated for Christmas, and the soft lighting. They had a candle lighting ceremony and a live nativity.

It was the time to get dressed up and sit with the rest of the town. He and Brenda had made plans to sit together. Since she had her car, she planned to drive. So, Brenda and Thomas and Tracy and Lloyd, were all riding together with her into the town.

Brenda looked so beautiful in her red dress with the white fuzzy trim. She could have been Santa's wife if she wasn't so young, maybe Santa's daughter, that made more sense. And he was being silly.

"You ladies look amazing. Lloyd and I are going to be the envy of the whole area," he said.

The women twirled and thanked him.

Tracy had on a holly green-colored dress. Tracy had a lot of curves to her. And Lloyd seemed to think they were made just for him. Thomas was pretty sure he hadn't made any move on her, but he saw Lloyd's eyes follow her everywhere she went. They were gonna be a couple of sad sacks when the ladies went back to school.

It was gonna be very lonely at the Rockin' K when they were gone.

They would go back to just being ranch hands, rather than helpers on the mine discovery team. Yeah, he wasn't looking forward to the engineers leaving, not one little bit.

He decided not to think about later but concentrate on now. He directed Brenda on how to get into town and where she should park. Everyone from the surrounding area came to this service so parking was going to be at a premium. But he had a few tricks up his sleeve and they managed to find a parking space not too far from the church. And not too far from the Grange, where the after party would be held.

Brenda took his arm as they walked the short distance to the church. He couldn't be more pleased to have her snuggled up next to him.

The church service started early, so that everybody could enjoy themselves at the party, and still get home before it got icy out. Plus, it got dark so quickly this time of year that they could have a candlelight service at five o'clock in the evening if they wanted to. They didn't start quite that early, but it wasn't a whole lot later.

Thomas led the way over to his favorite pew, where they had a good view of the stage. "This is one of the best seats in the house. We want to be able to see the stage and the aisles."

Brenda batted her lashes at him. "You're the boss, Thomas."

He chuckled. "Not me, but I have been to this a time or two. It's one of my favorite Christmas events."

The church filled up quickly, until every seat was taken, and a few men and teenage boys stood at the back. He'd stood back there a number of times when there had been a need for an extra seat.

The service started with the reading of Luke. And as each passage was read. Different people appeared to act out the reading. There were some songs interspersed, like 'Away in a Manger' and other favorites. Then they turned off the lights and held the candle lighting ceremony. During the candle lighting part was when the baby appeared in the manger. So that when all the candles were finally lit all through the church, they could see the baby Jesus. At the very end they sang 'Silent Night' together. It was always a moving experience in his opinion. He'd always enjoyed it, even as a child.

When they were done singing, the lights came back up and they all wandered out, leaving their candles in the baskets at the back of the church. They all walked over as a crowd, to the Grange Hall, where the party would be held.

There were drinks and cookies to get them started. The music was fun Christmas songs, 'Rudolf the Red Nosed Reindeer', 'Frosty the Snowman' and other favorites. When 'Santa Claus is Coming to Town' came on it signaled the time for everyone to get settled.

The children all sat on the floor around a woman that was dressed up to look like Santa's wife. She read 'The Night Before Christmas' and at the end of the story Santa came in with a big bag of toys, and handed them out to the kids. They were simple toys, like balls, dolls, toy trucks, blocks, games, and the like. Mrs. Santa handed out candy canes that had googly eyes and pipe cleaner antlers to make them look like reindeers.

When all the toys were handed out Santa sat next to his wife and they had a cookie with the kids. And when they left, it signaled that the party was over, and everyone put their trash away. The Grange ladies packed up the leftovers.

Some of the men from town would stay to help clean up any mess. Do the sweeping, help rinse out the coffee pots and pitchers from the drinks. Mostly it was people without families, whether they were young, or whether they were old, there was always cooperation.

Normally he would stay and help, but since he was with Brenda, and the Kiplings had plans after this party he went with them. When they got back to the ranch, a spread of protein and vegetables were laid out, something to counteract the sugar of the candy and cookies.

And then they all sat around for their traditional Christmas Eve package opening, each person had one package that they would open. Thomas knew that usually it was a pair of pajamas, and a book. He didn't really expect to have one. But he knew he'd enjoy watching the others.

Travis brought in the big bag that had just those gifts in them. Tony asked if he could help pass them out. Travis laughed and said, "Of course, you can."

Travis took each gift, out of the bag, read off the name and handed it to Tony. Thomas saw the joy on the boy's face as he ran around giving out the gifts. Thomas was surprised when both he and Lloyd got one, as well as all the engineers, he probably shouldn't have been, he'd been working for the family his whole life.

Brenda and Tracy looked surprised, just as surprised as he felt. The tradition was to open their gifts, and then put on those new pajamas and watch a movie together. He had no idea what kind of movie it would be, whether it was a funny kid's movie or an old-fashioned movie or what, but he opened his pajamas and found a book from one of his favorite authors.

He glanced up when he heard a gasp, it was Tracy with her hand over her mouth, looking down into her package that she'd ripped open, she choked out a thank you, thrust her gift to Brenda, jumped up, and ran out of the room.

Brenda started to stand to go after her.

Lloyd said, "No, stay here Brenda, I'll do it." And he followed Tracy out.

Brenda didn't know what to say exactly, but everyone was looking worried, so she said, "Tracy grew up in foster homes. I think you including her, and your gift means a lot to her, and she's a little overwhelmed by her emotions. So, don't take it as a bad thing."

The Kipling's all nodded. Some of the women looked like they wanted to break down in tears.

Travis said, "Let's get changed and meet back down here in twenty minutes for the movie."

So, they swallowed away their tears and everyone split off to go change into their pajamas. Brenda took Tracy's package up to her room, with her own.

A little bit later Tracy came into Brenda's room. "I'm sorry I got up and ran away. I was just..."

Brenda hugged her roommate, "It's okay. Don't worry."

"Do you think I made too big a fool of myself to go down and enjoy the movie?"

Brenda shook her head. "Absolutely not. Everyone will be happy to have you there."

"Did you say anything?"

"I just told them that you had been raised in foster homes, and maybe were a little stunned by their generosity."

Tears leaked out of her eyes. "Oh, thank you. That's exactly it, you know. I cried all over poor Lloyd, he just patted my back and let me blubber."

"He'll be fine. We've been friends for a long time, Tracy. Now go wash your face and no more crying."

The girls changed into their pajamas and went downstairs together.

As soon as they walked in the room, Tony jumped up and ran to Tracy and hugged her around the waist. "Miss Tracy I'm so glad you came back to watch the movie with us. You look very pretty in your pajamas."

Tracy laughed and Brenda knew that everything was going to be okay. Brenda and Tracy angled over to where Lloyd, and Thomas sat and snuggled down with them, to watch the movie.

CHAPTER 17

Christmas morning Brenda and Tracy again went to help feed the animals in the barn. Everyone started early. And she found out that Tony wasn't allowed to come downstairs. Until his parents came to get him. But he had a new book to read.

Brenda realized that this was part of the point of the Christmas Eve gifts, to give Tony, and any other children, something to do in the morning, while the family took care of the needs of the animals. Breakfast was just going to be the family today, including Lloyd and Thomas, so they'd be sitting around the table for breakfast, which proved to be monkey bread, frittata, and some breakfast meats.

After they'd eaten. They went into the family room, to open gifts. Brenda was very happy with the fact that she had gifts for everyone. And she'd put both her and Tracy's name on them.

Tracy hugged her when she'd pointed it out. "Thank you so much for letting me be a part of it."

"It's my pleasure. You're my BFF, you know, besides it's just a little token."

Brenda was surprised, after all the gifts were handed out, to find she had quite a lap full. She knew hers and Tracy's were not down here. It seemed like she had gifts from almost everyone.

She had one from Tony, that he'd made at Rachel's house, and one that had Thomas's name on it, and one from each of the families. Tracy was staring open mouthed at the pile in her own lap. Tracy and Brenda were sitting side by side with Lloyd on the other side of Tracy and Thomas on the other side of Brenda.

Brenda noticed Tracy looking at her, giving her a sheepish smile and took her hand. Tracy laid her head on her shoulder.

Tracy whispered. "I've never gotten so many gifts at the same time. Except from you. I don't know how to act."

Brenda whispered back. "Just open them, smile, and say thank you."

"But it's too much."

Brenda had to agree with that, but it wouldn't help Tracy. "No, it's not. It's just one small gift from each family. We're here to help them and they're grateful that we took our holiday and came. So, don't be concerned. Just open them, smile, and say thank you."

"Okay, I'll try."

The one from Tony was one of the ones Brenda was most excited about. She opened it, and found it was a frame made out of popsicle sticks. And the picture in the frame was of Tony in a huge apron with a mixing spoon in his hand, and a bowl in front of him. It had the year written on the frame by hand at the top, and his name, Tony McCoy, handwritten at the bottom.

"Oh Tony, it's wonderful, thank you so much."

Nearly everyone in the room expressed similar sentiments, apparently Tony's gift had been the first one everyone had opened.

The little boy beamed with pride. "Aunt Rachel helped me with it. She took my picture. The ribbon is to let it hang on your tree."

Brenda was impressed the boy had given credit to his aunt. He was going to be an amazing man when he grew up, some woman would be extremely lucky in twenty or thirty years.

She knew she wouldn't be saving it only for Christmas, she was going to hang it in her room, it would be one of her prized possessions. Something to remember this visit by.

The rest of the gifts were very nice, somewhat generic, female gifts. Some pretty soaps with columbines in them, a necklace with little bits of gold inside a glass container. Some perfume made from a local flower. A little bowl that would hold jewelry or some trinkets. Soft winter gloves, a scarf, and a hat that matched. So obviously, several of the women had gotten together and bought matching things. She thanked each one as she opened them.

The gift from Grandpa K surprised her, it was a compass, she looked up to see him watching her. "To guide you back to us someday."

Her smile wobbled as she fought the tears. "Thank you so much Grandpa K. I will come back. I promise."

"See that you do."

Everyone called out a thank you for their box of chocolates. Katie had clued her in that the whole family and all the ranch hands had a chocolate addiction. She'd helped her order enough for everyone from one of her suppliers. So, Brenda had a box for each person on the ranch, whether they were here this morning or not.

Brenda had opened all her gifts except for the one from

Thomas. She'd watched as the other engineers had gotten gifts from Thomas. He'd done very well in picking out things. She had let the anticipation build before opening hers. It was heavy, but not very big, maybe a foot by six inches. Only a couple of inches tall. She looked at him and he winked at her, and she started to tear the paper off of it. When she got the paper torn off, she laughed at the picture on the box.

"You got me a chess set?"

"I did. It's a traveling one, the pieces all fit inside, and the box shuts and latches."

"But it's heavy because it's made out of quartz."

"I figured the geologist needed rocks for her chess set."

She laid her head on his shoulder, so he couldn't see that her eyes had filled. "Thank you."

"It's a little selfish in that I wanted you to remember me by it."

"I will, forever. Thank you so much."

～

THOMAS WAS GOING TO MISS THIS, MOSTLY BRENDA, BUT also being included in so many activities with the Kipling family. Things would go back to normal when the engineers left, Lily and Drew would be back in Wyoming, Emma and Zach off to the next rodeo, Lily's family back to their own lives in Montana

Thomas was content to sit with Brenda, with her head on his shoulder. His arm wrapped around her. But he knew there was more to come. He'd seen Zach get up a few minutes ago and quietly walk outside.

Thomas knew what was coming. So as other people also, quietly got up and walked out, he watched Tony play with his new toy horse.

Brenda started to say, "There's a horse just like—"

He squeezed her, to get her to stop. She looked up at him, and he shook his head slightly. Then he leaned down and whispered. "Don't say anything. But get Patricia and Steve's attention we all need to go outside."

She looked at him with wide eyes, and he winked at her. She leaned over to her friend. "Something's happening outside, just quietly get up and walk out."

Tracy nodded and went with Lloyd toward the back door. Brenda caught the eye of Patricia. She gave her head a little jerk towards the door. Patricia nudged her husband. And they quietly got up and walked to the door as well.

There were only a few people left in the room. Alyssa and Beau and their little daughter, Emily. Emma, Tony, and Grandpa K were busy keeping Tony occupied with his new horse. Brenda and Thomas stood to go join the rest of the people out in the yard.

They went to the mudroom, Thomas whispered, "Tony's getting a new horse for Christmas. The one you saw."

"Oh, how fun."

He heard Tony say, "Where did everybody go?"

Emma said, "Oh just out in the yard. Let's go see what they're looking at, okay?"

He heard the rest of them moving toward the mud room and hustled Brenda out the door. He heard Emma say. "No wear your cowboy boots, Tony."

"But Mama it's snowy, snow boots are for snow."

"It's okay, wear your cowboy boots."

"Okay, Mama."

They were all gathered around three horses. The one that looked like Tony had gotten a toy of and two of Zach's horses. Brenda and Thomas joined them, some of the ranch

CHRISTMAS AT THE ROCKIN' K

hands were in the circle also, grinning like crazy. Everyone couldn't wait to see Tony get his first full-sized horse.

Beau and Alyssa came out the door first with Emily on Alyssa's hip. She was still little enough to carry. And they hadn't stopped to put shoes on her. Grandpa K came out with a big grin on his face.

Finally, Emma and Tony came out. Tony said, "That horse looks just like my toy."

Emma said, "Yes it does. Can you guess why?"

Tony frowned. "Nope. But that's yours and daddy's horses next to it. Are we going for a ride? Do I get to ride that horse?"

"As a matter of fact, yes, we are going to go for a ride. You, me, and Daddy."

"What's the horse's name?" Tony asked.

"He doesn't have one yet."

"Why not? That's sad, horses need a name." Thomas glanced at Brenda who was looking sad, so he winked at her.

"He doesn't have a name yet, because you need to name him," Emma explained.

"Me."

"Yep."

"Why me?" he frowned.

"Because he's your new horse, Tony."

He looked up at his mother, confusion on his face. "My new horse?"

"Yep. Your last Christmas present."

"Really? Are you sure?" Tony looked around at all the family gathered, all of whom were nodding with big grins on their faces. Thomas knew his grin was as big as everyone else's. The last place Tony looked was to his father. Zach was holding the reins of all three horses, but nodded to his son.

Tony let out a whoop and ran over to hug his horse, but

then stopped and let the horse smell him, as he'd been taught. "Oh, I am so happy. You're going to be my horse. I will think of a very good name for you."

A frown flickered over his face, and he asked his dad, "What are we going to do about my pony?"

Zach said. "I thought maybe you'd want to give it to Emily."

Tony thought about that for a moment, then nodded. "Okay, Emily can have him. He's a good pony. But I'm ready for my own big horse."

"Yes, we thought you were old enough and mature enough to handle a new horse, a full-size horse."

Tony looked around at all his family. "You all knew I was getting a horse for Christmas, didn't you? That's why I was watching Emily, when I normally help feed the horses."

They all nodded and laughed.

Tony looked at Lily's mom and dad. "Is this one of your horses?"

"Yes, Tony, it is," said Howard.

"Yay. You have very good horses. Daddy said so."

Thomas could see Howard trying not to laugh, the kid was just so darn cute. "We hope you have many years enjoying him."

"I know I will." He rushed over and gave Howard a hug, and then Elaine. Then he went around the circle and hugged everyone else.

Thomas could see that both Brenda and Tracy were near tears and he wondered why such simple things affected them so strongly. He was going to have to get to the bottom of this.

When Tony had hugged everyone, he said. "Let's ride him first and I will think of the name while we're riding."

Emma laughed. "I think that's a very good idea."

Then he raced back over to the horse. "Mama, can you give me a boost, he's a little bit tall for me to get on."

"Sure thing."

"I'll do that," Grandpa K said.

"Okay thanks, Grandpa K." He boosted the little guy up until he could get his foot in the stirrup and swing onto the saddle.

He took the reins from his father. "Thanks, Daddy. Thanks, Mommy."

Zach said, "You just hold on right there so your mom and I can get on our horses and we'll take your new horse out for a nice ride."

Tony leaned forward to pat his new horse on the neck. "Okay, I'll just pet him."

Once Emma and Zach were on their horses, the family moved to the side so that the three of them could take their horses on a ride,

CHAPTER 18

The next day the exploration crew set out to go back to searching for the mine. It was cold and still a little icy in places, but Brenda's ankle seemed to be fine. She'd wrapped it and then pulled on her hiking boots. She'd been walking around on it now for a couple of days with no trouble, no crutches, and best of all, no pain. Thomas had assured her that there wouldn't be much ice where they were going, since there hadn't been any human interference to cause a fast melt like around the house.

They were finally going to start up the ravine she'd found, and she felt a little giddy at the prospect and hoped she wasn't steering them in the wrong direction, but the samples they'd tested seemed to verify her idea.

Lloyd led the horses back out to take to the cabin, since they might actually start using them now that they knew which direction they were headed. They would be going up the ravine and that wasn't as easy on foot as the mostly flat pasture had been.

They'd talked about spending a night or two at the cabin,

so they didn't have to take the time each day to travel back and forth.

Thomas had said, "The cabin can certainly hold six people, it can hold ten with the foldout couch."

"But it's really setup for a bunch of guys," Brenda explained. "There are two sets of bunk beds in one room. Two double beds in another. And the foldout couch, so unless we had a boy's room and a girl's room it wouldn't work easily."

The main people that idea would affect was Patricia and Steve, they wouldn't be able to sleep together unless they took the fold-out couch.

Patricia said, "It's only a few minutes' drive."

Steve looked relieved. "Yeah, let's just go on as we have been."

Brenda wasn't the least bit sad for that decision, she thought of the cabin as her and Thomas's space. It might be silly of her, but it was what it was.

They took the vehicles over as close as they could get to where they wanted to start looking. They hadn't driven across the contaminated field until they had it completely mapped out. But now that they had it mapped out, they could drive right up to the spot where Brenda had twisted her ankle.

They started up the ravine taking samples as they went. When they got to a fork, they would go in a few yards, take some samples, and label those carefully. Then continue back up. It was tedious work. But they needed to know which direction to go once they had tested all the branches.

They kept going higher and higher, and still hadn't gotten very far on the map that they had to go by. At night they went back to the house and did the testing, happy to be able to mark off the tributaries. Those side branches had no contamination in them, if they went in far enough to test.

But in the main ravine, they were following the contamination and it got stronger the farther up they went, it took them five days to get to the top. They decided to go all the way to the road, taking samples as they went. Then they tested the contamination strength so they could pinpoint it on the map, where the contamination stopped. Each day they could take the horses to the previous day's stopping point, but they had to tether them away from the contaminated grass. Once the horses were secure, they would keep going on foot, to be able to take continual samples.

And they knew the mine, or at least the processing area had to be in the area with the largest concentration of cyanide poisoning. Above that would be uncontaminated. So, they finally had it pinned down to what looked like a small area on the map. But in reality, she knew it was a large space since they would expand from there.

Now that they knew where they were going, they could start taking the horses up and leave them in the uncontaminated area and search on foot for the mine. But that would start after New Year's Day, because tomorrow was New Year's Eve.

The horses could stay at the cabin, since Brenda and Thomas would be there to take care of them. She'd been so excited when Thomas had told her that they would be able to spend New Year's Eve and New Year's Day at the cabin. And she could hardly wait.

He told her he had to do chores in the morning of the 31st, and then they could go to the cabin about one. She was eagerly looking forward to it.

The house had emptied out with everyone returning to their lives in other states. Tony and his family would be back to load up their horses a few days before they would leave to go back to school. She was glad she'd see him one more time and he would fill the house with noise. It was quiet now with only the seven of them rattling around in it.

∼

Thomas went into town on New Year's Eve morning to pick up a few things for his night with Brenda. He wanted to romance her a bit.

He had to go to several different places to pick up everything he wanted for New Year's Eve. He had to go to the liquor store to get the champagne, and he went to Katie's to get the chocolates, and the New Year's Eve fun things, like party hats and noisemakers, and condoms, he didn't know how many were in the 'girl box', and decided he wouldn't want to use them all up, anyway. It wasn't easy finding flowers this time of the year, but he'd managed to do so. He'd ordered them from Granby and had asked them to be delivered to Katie's store, she'd been perfectly fine with that. Finally, he went by the cafe and picked up the meal that he'd ordered, so he wouldn't have to spend time cooking, or Brenda either, for that matter.

He ran around picking up all the different things that he'd ordered and then took them back to the cabin to get it ready for Brenda. She thought he was doing chores around the ranch this morning. But what he was really doing was getting the cabin ready for their night together. He wanted it to be special. She'd be going back to school in a little over a week now. And that would be the end of it.

Even though the school was only a couple of hours away, he had decided to break it off with her when she left. She was young and had her whole life ahead of her. And she needed to be free to pick a man that would suit her. He didn't think he was ever going to love anyone the way he loved her. He hadn't even realized he'd loved her until he started thinking about the future. And he just couldn't see himself with anyone else.

But that didn't mean he could saddle her with on old ranch hand, so he'd set her free. And remember in the years to come, that he'd held the bright, vivacious, and very intelligent woman in his arms.

Once he set everything up, he hoped that he would be able to dazzle her a little bit, just a little bit. He wanted her to remember him. Maybe when she saw a chess game, or had champagne at midnight on another New Year's Eve, he would pop back into her mind and she would smile.

CHAPTER 19

Thomas had the cabin as ready as he could make it and went to the bunk house to do the same with his person. A shower, a shave, and his best clothes. His best jeans, best shirt, a string tie, his best boots, and a cowboy hat. He walked across the yard to the door, knocked once, and went in, Meg was in the kitchen.

She turned to him when he walked in and looked him up and down. "Well now Thomas, don't you look nice?"

He felt a little awkward seeing the woman that had been his surrogate mother most of his life, knowing she knew he was taking Brenda out to the cabin. "Thanks."

Meg said, "Travis said you and Brenda are going to have a little New Year's Eve celebration out in cabin two."

He felt a quick bite of embarrassment and squelched it as best he could. "Yes, ma'am."

"Well, that's just fine then. But you're welcome in the house anytime. You don't have to hide out at cabin two to be with the lady."

"Travis mentioned you would be okay with that. But I wanted to wait until the house was a little bit less full. I don't think Brenda would be embarrassed. But we didn't need to broadcast it either."

"Well, everyone's gone now. Tony, Emma, and Zack will be back for a night or two later this week, before they head to Denver. But all the rest of the family members are back in their own lives again. The house feels empty now." Meg said with a sigh, loneliness covered her like a blanket. He could only imagine what she felt with so many of her kids off living their lives in other places.

"It does. But it was good to have everyone here for Christmas."

"Yes. It was a fine time." She smiled with the warm memories. "And they'll be back when they can. Do you want me to call Brenda down or do you want to go up?"

He decided he'd go up, other than to carry in her luggage, he hadn't been up to her room since she'd moved in. "I'll go on up, Meg."

"Well, have a good time for new year. Don't hurry back tomorrow."

"Thanks, Meg."

Thomas went up the stairs, it made him feel a little nervous to be going to pick up his date for New Year's. But he was excited at the same time. He rapped on her door. She answered it, and she looked amazing. He froze in place and couldn't think a single thought, not even what to say.

Brenda smiled at him. "Well now don't you look handsome. I take it you like my outfit."

His brain kicked into gear enough to mutter, "Like, is a very lame word for what I feel about your outfit."

Her eyes sparkled. "Excellent."

Finally, he got his brain and mouth to work together. "Brenda, you look very beautiful, amazingly sexy, you take my breath away. So, let's get out of here before I push you back into your room and have my way with you right here in the house. I've a hankering to strip you out of that pretty dress to see what's under it."

Her eyes heated and she licked her lips. "I wouldn't argue with that."

He wanted to take her up on that, but not now. First, he wanted to romance her a bit. "Another time. Let's go, pretty lady."

He took the bag she'd packed in one hand and her hand in the other and they went together down the wide stairs and out into the yard where he'd parked the truck. It was afternoon and still bright out, but evening fell quickly this time of year and he wanted as much time as he could get for their getaway.

∽

Brenda was more than happy to take Thomas's hand and let him lead her off for their adventure. She wondered about his "Another time" statement, but decided to wait to ask until they were on their way.

Brenda let Thomas guide her to the truck, open the door for her, and help her to slide in. Before he shut the door. He glanced down at the short skirt that had ridden up her legs. And then he kissed her hard and fast and shut the door. She was stunned by the fierceness of the kiss.

He slid in next to her. Her skin humming from the pleasure of his kiss. Her blood heating, she was thankful the drive was only a few minutes. She needed to calm down, so she didn't explode. So, she dug deep for what the question she'd had before he kissed her. Oh right, that 'another time' comment.

"So, what did you mean by 'another time'?"

He looked at her with a dumbfounded expression.

"You said you wanted to push me back into my room and have your way with me and I said that would be great and you said 'another time'."

"Oh, right. Well, both Travis and Meg have pointed out to me that I don't have to sneak you off to cabin two, that I'm welcome to join you in your room, if that's what you want."

"Really?"

"Yeah."

"That's excellent. When did they say that?"

"Meg, just tonight as I was coming to pick you up. Travis told me a few days ago when I asked him about using cabin two."

"A few days ago?" Why hadn't he mentioned that before now? They could have been enjoying each other all this time. "Why didn't you say anything before?" She could hear the petulance in her voice.

"I wanted to wait till there wasn't so many people in the house."

"Oh, well, I suppose that's okay." But she didn't feel okay, she felt grumpy he hadn't wanted her.

He took hold of her hand. "I just don't want it to be a thing of gossip, I want it to be something special between the two of us."

"Oh." She could feel her eyes, turning into hearts as she looked at him

"I wanted to have this special time with you. A little something special for just us".

Were there hearts circling around her head? She certainly felt like there could have been, or stars, or maybe bluebirds singing. She was getting ridiculous. This was a short-term affair. And she didn't need to go falling in love with him.

She only had another ten days on the ranch, if that, before

they'd be heading back to school. It made her heart sad to think of that. She enjoyed him. She enjoyed the family. There wasn't anything about the ranch she didn't like, but she had another semester to get through to earn her doctorate.

Brenda wasn't about to derail that. So, she'd enjoy her next ten days with him. She would enjoy her next ten days at the ranch. Meg had said that Tony would be back through for a day or two before they left, and she would enjoy seeing Tony again. And then after that, she would put this time of fun away and go back to her real life. And if the vision of that was a little bit dull? She would get used to it.

They pulled up to cabin two. Thomas came around to open her door and help her slide out. Her dress was short enough that if he didn't it might end up around her waist. Not that he wouldn't enjoy the vision of her fancy underwear, but she was saving that for later. He grabbed her suitcase out of the backseat of the truck. And she wondered why he didn't have anything of his own, just her overnight bag. But it didn't really matter.

He was pulling her along towards the cabin. He opened the door, and she could feel the warmth.

"It's already warm," she said.

"Yeah, I came by and started a fire."

She walked in, and her mouth dropped open. Not only had he started a fire, but there were roses on the table, and in the living room, and she wondered if there were some in the bedroom as well. There was a bottle of champagne in a bucket that wasn't really an ice bucket, but it was full of ice and champagne. In the living room there were party hats and noisemakers she figured were for midnight.

"You went to so much trouble for me," she whispered. No one had ever fussed over her like this.

"It was no trouble. I wanted to bring something a little special for tonight."

"Oh, you did." She stepped up to him, put her arms around his neck and pulled his head down to her so she could give him a kiss. A warm luscious kiss that lasted a long time.

He had one arm around her, the other one holding her bag. She pulled back, "Put that bag down."

He did so, and she pulled his head back down for another kiss, this one was hotter, more passion, more flair. More lust.

He dragged her to him. His hands fisting in the back of her dress like he wanted to tear it off of her. She pretty much felt the same way about his clothes. But she liked the dress, and she didn't want it torn off. So, when she pulled back a second time, she slipped the straps over her arms and let the dress fall to her feet.

While he was busy gawking, taking in the little scraps of underwear she had on. She started unbuttoning his shirt, and pulled the string tie off. Yanked the shirt out of the waistband of his pants, and pushed it off his shoulders, until it joined her dress on the floor.

She ran her hands over his chest and hummed in pleasure.

He drew her back to him, pulled her up to her toes, and beyond to where their mouths would meet, she wrapped her legs around his waist. She couldn't get close enough.

He devoured her mouth, and she reveled in the glory. He carried her down the hall to the bedroom, where there were indeed more flowers. They sank into the bed, his hands roaming her skin. Hers were on his back, he was so strong and muscular, her fingers dug in.

He supped at her body, down her neck, around her collarbone, on her shoulders. Kissing, licking, nibbling down to her breasts. He kissed the soft flesh above the lace, then took her nipple into his mouth. The lace was causing incredible sensations, with his hot mouth on the other side. She shivered and gripped the sheets of the bed.

"Thomas."

"Yes, baby."

"Thomas, I need you."

"You've got me, I'm right here." The vibration of his mouth streaked through her body.

"No, naked, inside."

He chuckled. But only switched to her other breast to tease it as he had the first. She tried to reach his belt. But her arms were too relaxed. She didn't have the strength to do much more than simply take whatever he gave her. He kissed his way down to her belly button, and kissed it, too, then licked a circle around it. His head moved lower. He started pulling her panties down with his teeth and she shuddered.

Never in her whole life, had she felt that kind of heat, then he stopped and licked her and she thought she might die from the pleasure. He spent several long minutes with his mouth on her, until she shattered from the sensations.

When he'd gotten the panties all the way down to her shoes, which she still had on, he pulled them off, and started unbuckling her shoes.

"These are so sexy, but they can't be comfortable. And I want you completely relaxed."

With another shudder, she forced herself up to unhook her bra and drop it on the other side of the bed. When the second shoe was dropped onto the floor, she said, "Now don't come back here until you're naked too."

He gave her a crooked grin and then started unbuckling his pants, toed out of his boots, and dropped everything onto the floor. Then he reached into the nightstand and pulled a string of condoms out of what looked to her like a new box, and laid them on the top of the nightstand. Then he joined her back in the bed.

She grabbed him, brought his mouth to hers and kissed him greedily. Her legs wrapping around his to hold him tight. Her hands reaching wanting to touch him everywhere. He fought back to touch her in kind. Sensations swirled through her body. A whirlwind, a fire storm, lightning, she couldn't take much more.

"Thomas. Now," she managed to croak out.

He stopped the torment for only a moment when he grabbed the condom, rolled it on and slid slowly inside her. Where the pleasure only built higher and higher. He moved in her, and she gloried in it. His hand went between them, his rough fingers found her already sensitive clit. It only took a little bit of movement on his part, before she was flying, flying on the storm, in the whirlwind.

He kept moving inside her. Slowly. She came back to herself. The tension started building again. She didn't know if she could take it a third time. But it kept building.

She sobbed out. "Come with me. Come with me."

And this time, they flew together in the whirlwind. And on the storm.

CHAPTER 20

Thomas lay shattered, desperately trying to get his breath back. He was smashing Brenda into the mattress, he needed to move but he had no energy. He had no strength. It was completely gone. The orgasm had wiped him clean, hollowed him out, it had been so extreme, so powerful.

It had been like trying to ride a wild mustang, power he couldn't control. He'd fought to control it. But he hadn't. And he didn't think she had either. He hooked his arm around her and rolled them. So, he was on his back, with her on top of him.

She sighed and took a deep breath, then curled up on him, her head on his chest. Her arms around him. Legs tangled with his. And they lay there together, trying to catch their breath. Their hearts thundering in unison. His hands ran up and down her back, skin so soft he needed to touch it, still warm from their lovemaking.

This woman had gotten under his skin. And he wasn't sure he was going to survive it when she left. They had ten days before that happened. And he was determined to take every bit of pleasure he could wring from those ten days, and give her as much love, as he could.

They lay there in the silence. The smell of roses drifting, which reminded him that they hadn't even opened the champagne. They'd been in too big of a hurry. He wasn't surprised at that. Their last night here, in this same cabin, had been almost two weeks ago

When his breathing was normal, and his heart rate regular, and his skin had cooled, he kissed the top of her head. "We haven't opened the champagne yet. And I have dinner for us that needs to be heated up."

She kissed his chest, raised up to look him in the eye. "Are you hungry?"

"Not particularly. I'm very happy here with you as my blanket. But I wanted to offer."

"I'm not hungry yet either. We can save the champagne for a little bit later. I just want to lay here in your arms."

"That's perfectly fine with me. I like you here in my arms."

She reached down and got the throw that was at the bottom of the bed and pulled it up over the top of them. They lay there in perfect contentment.

Before they got up to have dinner, they made love another time. This time it was slow and gentle, but no less satisfying.

When their hunger forced them out of bed, Brenda took his shirt and put it on. It hit her, almost at her knees, and she had to roll the sleeves up, but he thought his shirt had never looked better. It was warm enough in the cabin for both of them to go barefoot and that seemed to make it more intimate.

He quickly put the food in the oven to heat and popped the cork on the champagne. While they waited for dinner to heat, they made toasts to twisted ankles and chess games and remote cabins. And neither one of them mentioned her going back to school soon. They ate the meal from the cafe, and it tasted better with the two of them sitting close together, sharing bites of food, and bites of their lives.

As the clock hands moved towards midnight, they turned music on the radio, and wore their party hats and danced and laughed. At midnight, they kissed for long minutes until they were both panting. He finally pulled back and handed her a noisemaker. And they popped them, streamers and confetti filled the air.

They drank more champagne and danced until the wee hours of the morning, then Brenda, took his hand and led him back to the bedroom where they made love again.

~

BRENDA WOKE WHEN THOMAS PULLED OUT OF HER ARMS.

"Where are you going?" she asked sleepily.

He kissed her forehead. "I need to go take care of the horses, then I'll be back. You just rest, it's still early. Go back to sleep."

She snuggled down into the blankets. She didn't think she was going to go back to sleep. But she'd be happy to lay in bed and think about her night with Thomas. It had been magical, not just the sex, but the fact that he'd prepared for their night together with champagne and dinner. He'd surprised her with the party hats and noisemakers. The radio and dancing had been lovely. She had never had a night so magical, so wonderful. She would never forget it.

She wanted to do something for him in return. So, while he was out taking care of the horses, she popped out of bed, pulled on some of the clothes that she'd brought with her, and went into the kitchen to cook him a breakfast fit for a king.

Well maybe not a king, since she wasn't that great of a cook. Neither she nor Tracy had been allowed in the kitchen. Brenda because they had a cook and Tracy because none of the foster homes had wanted to teach her. She and Tracy had lived in the dorms and eaten at the cafeteria their first few years, but then they'd gotten the bright idea to move to their own place.

Which had been marvelous, until they realized neither one of them could cook. They could still eat at the cafeteria, but now that they were 'off campus' it wasn't as convenient, and they'd decided it was high time they learned to cook. They were intelligent women after all, how hard could it be?

So, they'd watched cooking shows and YouTube videos and experimented. The first few times had been such disasters Brenda had considered hiring a cook or meal service. But they'd buckled down and were determined to learn. And they had. Neither of them would ever be world class chefs, but they could feed themselves, dammit.

She started the coffee, found bacon and eggs, and decided to make pancakes to go with them, when she found the pancake mix. She didn't know how long it would take him with the horses, whether he was just feeding them or whether he would muck out their stalls, also.

But she figured she could put it all in the oven to keep warm if he didn't come in right away. She started with the bacon. Then while the bacon was cooking, she mixed up pancake batter. She'd do the eggs last just because they didn't sit so well. Reheated pancakes would be fine, and the bacon would be fine, she'd do the eggs when he walked in. With a mountain of bacon and at tower of pancakes in the oven, she was ready. The coffee was made, and she'd set the table. They could use the rest of the champagne to make mimosas. She'd add the champagne when he came in, there wasn't much left.

When she heard his boots on the steps, she poured the eggs into the pan. Scrambled eggs, nothing fancy.

When he came into the kitchen, he said, "Something smells good."

"I made you breakfast."

He came up and nuzzled her neck. "I think you smell better than the breakfast."

She stirred the eggs and then turned her head to give him a kiss. Just a light one. "Eat first, while the food is warm. And you can munch on me later."

He chuckled. "I'll go get washed up then."

While he was doing that, she pulled the food out of the oven, set it on the table, spooned the eggs into a serving bowl, took cups of coffee over, and poured the champagne into the orange juice.

When he came back, he kissed her neck. "Thanks for making breakfast."

She smiled. "Thanks for making last night so special. I'll remember it always."

"So will I." Then he sat. "Wow this looks great. You made pancakes."

"I did, something special for New Year's Day."

He filled this plate, and picked up his mimosa, they clinked glasses together. "To the New Year. May it be prosperous and filled with joy."

She swallowed hard. She didn't think it was going to be filled with joy once she left the ranch, but she didn't want to let on, so she smiled and drank, then forced herself to eat while they talked.

They'd arranged for the rest of the crew to meet them at the cabin on the day after New Year's Day. That gave them two nights at the cabin, instead of just one. And they enjoyed every minute of it.

They spent the rest of the day and night, in each other's arms, trying to have a lifetime of togetherness in a few hours.

CHAPTER 21

*T*he next morning, they made love as the sun came up, it was time to get back to work. They cleaned up the cabin and got it ready for the next time someone used it. It wouldn't be them. They wouldn't be back. It made her sad to think about that, so she pushed it to the back of her mind.

They washed the towels and sheets and anything else they'd used. Got the cabin spick and span and ready. They put their personal belongings in the backseat of the truck Thomas had driven out.

When the rest joined them, they took the horses, now that they knew how far up they needed to go, and where it was safe to tether them.

So, they rode the horses up carrying the survey equipment with them. They hoped they would find the mine and they could map it out. It took them five days to find it. Five days of searching from sunup to sunset. In the evenings Thomas and she spent the time in her room playing chess, and making love.

Brenda found it the most satisfying five days of her life.

Working hard during the day. Loving hard at night. When they finally found the mine that they'd walked past at least a couple of times, they laughed. It was set up in a way that you couldn't see the entrance. Someone had planted trees right in front of it. They would nearly need to squeeze by the trees to get into the mine.

They'd actually found tailings before they found the mine.

Steve squatted down. "This looks like it's been disturbed recently."

Thomas nodded, "I have to agree with that. I see both evidence of bear, and possibly a human. The weather hasn't helped to preserve evidence."

"No," Steve said, "I don't think it's weather causing the trouble, bears maybe, but I kind of doubt it's only wildlife. I think we can shore up this place here to keep the contamination from running downhill, until we can get the mine reclamation team in here."

"That would be good." Thomas said

Lloyd pointed out, "There were some pretty decent rocks up the hill a way that we could haul down here to shore it up. Maybe get some quick dry cement to put in between the rocks."

Steve nodded. "That would work. We've got a few days to get that started, before we have to get back to school. I'd kind of like to take a look in the mine as well."

Thomas said, "Yeah, we can do that, but I want to have a look first before we disturb anything inside. Since the weather wouldn't have gotten to it there might be something to find out what's going on."

"Fair enough. Let's go get some of those rocks. We can start hauling down some of them."

"We've got quick dry cement at the ranch. So, we could

bring that up tomorrow, start laying the rocks down," Lloyd said.

Brenda wasn't a huge fan of carrying rocks. But she would do what was necessary.

Steve said, "Patricia, Tracy, why don't you start the survey, while the rest of us go up and start getting rocks."

Brenda knew that Steve was keeping Patricia from carrying too much, plus she and Tracy worked well together. Steve didn't do or say a whole lot about the pregnancy, since Patricia was a fiercely independent woman. The survey was needed. And she and Tracy could do it.

Patricia nodded. Even Brenda had seen the look in Steve's eyes of fierceness that was not going to be brooked. Brenda was glad that Patricia had relented. She was a strong woman, but she was nearing forty, it was her first child, and was due in less than twelve weeks. So, a little bit of caution was in order.

Patricia and Tracy walked with them back to where the horses were to get the survey equipment off of them. While the rest of them went up the hill a bit, where they had seen a tumble of rocks.

Thomas said, "Let's just take a few down to get started. We've got some equipment that would help to haul more rocks down, we can bring it out tomorrow."

Steve nodded. "That sounds like a good plan, carrying rocks up and down a hill is not exactly my choice of entertainment."

Brenda couldn't keep it in, she said, "This isn't entertainment, boss. This is a job."

He chuckled. "So, do you want to do it by hand, Brenda?"

"Hell no. Let's get that equipment up here."

The four of them carried down what they could and set them on the edge where the breach was. When they got back from the second load, Patricia and Tracy were nearly finished with the outside survey.

"Once you have a chance to look inside, Thomas, we'll do an internal survey as well," Patricia said.

"Did anyone bring a flashlight with them?" he asked.

All of them shook their heads.

"Well then, I guess it'll be tomorrow. We need to start heading back down now, anyway."

Dinner that night turned into a celebration. The minute Steve had announced they'd found the mine, calls were made to the four Kipling siblings in their own houses, to bring whatever dinner they had prepared and join the family at the big house to hear the news.

Brenda and Tracy helped Meg add another three side dishes.

Meg said, "I made a roast today, since Emma and her family are picking up the horses. I thought any leftovers would make sandwiches, but with the impending crowd I doubt there will be any."

"But if they all bring their own food…" Brenda began.

Meg shook her head. "Alyssa and Beau hadn't started dinner yet; they'd just gotten cleaned up from working on an animal that had gotten hurt. The twins were planning to go get pizza, to pamper their pregnant ladies."

"Oh, well that only leaves Adam and Rachel."

Meg nodded, "Fortunately, Rachel was just taking a large lasagna out of the oven. She'd planned to freeze at least half of it, but I doubt there will be a scrap left, her lasagna is delicious."

Patricia joined them in time to carry out the food. She'd rested for a few minutes when the men had put the leaves in the table and then set out the place settings, and the women had gotten the food ready. Brenda was glad Patricia rested, she didn't indulge in such things often, but looking for the mine had been long days and strenuous climbing at times. Carrying a child due in only a couple of months while engaging in such activity couldn't be easy.

When everyone was gathered around the table Travis stood at the head, with a glass of champagne. "I'd like to toast the engineers and helpers. Today they found the mine causing us trouble."

They all raised their glasses, some of which held sparkling apple juice.

"Here, here," they said, and drank.

Brenda felt the flush of pleasure as they celebrated. She was proud to have been a part of the solution.

After the food had been passed and plates filled, Travis cleared his throat to silence the room. "Steve, give us the run down."

Steve grinned and Brenda felt so proud of them all. "We haven't been inside the mine yet, so we don't know how big it is. But we found the contamination source and it looked like it had been disturbed recently rather than nature having caused it."

Thomas continued, "There were clearly bear tracks, but I think under those were boot prints. I plan to take some lights up tomorrow to look in the cave for anything else we might find."

"We want to take some quick dry cement and make a rock wall to shore up the place. Then I can get and RFP out to see if we can't get some bids. I think it will work with the microbe technology rather than a full water treatment plant. It's not large enough to warrant that."

"RFP?" Katie asked.

"Request for proposal. I think it will probably be a six-to-eight-month project. We carried a few rocks down from further uphill to contain the runoff, but we'll need a lot more."

Travis said, "I think the four-wheeler and the small trailer would work to transport the rocks. I'll be joining you tomorrow."

"As will I," Grandpa K said. Several others said they planned to join them, also.

They discussed logistics for a few more minutes. Brenda marveled at how quiet Tony had been, listening to every word and calmly eating his dinner.

When the conversation about the mine was complete, Meg said, "Tony, you've been very patient. Tell us about your second Christmas."

The boy's eyes lit with excitement and his words flowed out like a river. Tony had enjoyed his second Christmas very much.

~

THE NEXT DAY IT WAS A DIFFERENT GROUP OF PEOPLE HEADED toward the mine. Grandpa K, Travis, Adam, and the twins joined them, they all wanted to see where it was. Travis had pulled a couple of ranch hands off working with the cattle to help build the wall. It wouldn't take very long with all those men helping.

Thomas had temporary lights that could be set up in the mine, as well as a flashlight. They had a four-wheeler, and a little trailer attached to it to haul the rocks, after leaving the bags of quick dry cement, and jugs of water to mix it with at the mine.

Thomas split off from the group, as soon as they got to the mine area, he took his flashlights and his portable lights with him. Starting in the mine he examined the ground, searching for evidence of who or what might be inside the mine. As he went further in, he found evidence of a bear that had been using this as his lair.

But he wasn't currently, there was a tangy odor on the air, over where the bear had occupied. Thomas wondered if it was bear repellent. If it was, that was evidence that a human had been in the cave and was trying to keep the bear out.

So, he started searching for more proof of humans in the cave. He searched farther and farther back, following the mine. He also looked carefully over where the rock had been mined, it all looked old nothing looked disturbed to him.

He needed to bring one of the engineers to have them look at it. But he wanted to search the whole area first, before he did that. As he got to the last wall. He found it did look a little different than the rest had, it was a little brighter. But he didn't find any other indication that there was anyone else that had been in here. Other than the one wall it all looked undisturbed, he decided it was time to bring an engineer back.

Maybe Patricia could tell him if what he was seeing was also what she saw.

As he was walking back, he noticed a little crevice that he hadn't seen from the other direction. There was barely room for a man to slip in sideways. But he followed it, and that's where he found evidence that clearly someone had been in here, and used it as a sleeping area. The ground had been leveled, smooth enough to accommodate a sleeping bag or even a blow-up mattress. There were also a couple of lanterns, battery-powered lanterns, which they certainly didn't have in the 1800s. Someone had been in there, recently.

CHAPTER 22

They'd worked hard for days. They'd gotten the contamination contained again, and Thomas had found evidence of recent inhabitation by a human. The mine was right on the property line between the Rockin' K and the national forest, a few steps uphill was National Forest, a few downhill, part of the Rockin' K. In fact, they had discovered that the mine was in the national forest and the tailings on the Rockin' K.

Mining was illegal either way, so they'd called in the authorities to have them look it over. There wasn't anything to do about it. Nobody was there now and there wasn't anything that they could track. But at least they knew why the contamination had occurred.

Brenda scowled, it was time to go back to school and she was not looking forward to it at all. She was going to miss Thomas. She'd decided to see if she could switch her schedule around so that she could come and visit for a few days each week. It was only a two-hour drive. If she could get Thursday and Friday clear. She'd have four days a week that she could be here. Even if she couldn't get it clear she could come for the weekends. She thought, maybe Tracy wouldn't mind coming on the weekends as well. She and Lloyd had a very strong friendship going, they could talk about it on the way back.

The next few days were going to be busy as they got ready for classes to resume. They needed to get groceries and settle back into their duplex. Get their books, or whatever else they might need for classes. So, she wouldn't be able to come back the next weekend. She'd be busy with school. But the weekend after she probably could.

She was packing up all of her clothes. Putting them into her suitcases, tidying up the room. She'd already stripped the sheets off the bed and had fresh ones on. She just needed to put the dirty ones in the hamper. Meg said that she would take care of getting them washed. Since all four of them were leaving she'd have a couple of loads of sheets to do, and towels.

They'd had a final dinner with everyone still on the ranch last night and had said their goodbyes. Steve had told them to expect a mine reclamation team in February or March and he'd call with more details when he had them.

There was a knock on her door, when she opened it, Thomas was there. "Thomas," she said delighted.

"I came to help you carry your luggage down."

"Oh, well thank you."

He walked in, shut the door behind him. "I want to talk to you."

She went up to him and pulled his head down and gave him a kiss.

He pulled away. "Yeah, I want to talk to you."

She laughed. "You said that already."

"Brenda. This has been a wonderful time. I'm so glad that

you came here for these three weeks. But I don't want you to be coming back. We need to go our separate ways."

"What?"

"I've been thinking about it. And I want you to find your place. You've got the last bit of school left. Then you'll be finding a job. And I don't want you to make any decisions around me. This has been one of the best times of my life. But we both knew it would be temporary."

Brenda didn't like the sound of this one bit. "But you're only two hours away."

"I know. I understand that. But I think it needs to be over."

"Well, I don't." Brenda insisted.

"You're young. You're beautiful. You've got your whole life ahead of you. I want you to go back to school and finish your degree, and then go to work for a company that's going to make you happy. Find someone your own age, maybe another engineer, you don't need some old cow hand on your mind."

"So, you just want me to walk away?"

"Yeah, it's best. You need to find your place."

Brenda was furious and sad at the same time. He didn't want her. He didn't want her! Well fine, she had her pride. She picked up her purse and backpack. She refused to let tears fall in front of him.

"Bring the luggage." She turned and stormed out the door and down the stairs. She was not going to cry. She was not, she refused. Tracy and Lloyd were waiting for her by her car so that they could put the luggage in. They loaded up the car and said their goodbyes. She didn't look at Thomas again.

She drove out of the ranch. Once they'd gotten about a mile down the road, Brenda pulled over. "You need to drive."

Tracy looked at her and said, "What happened?"

Brenda gulped back a sob. "Thomas broke up with me. He says I need to find my place."

"Men are so stupid."

"Yes, they are. But you need to drive."

They got out and met at the back of the car. Tracy hugged her tight. "I'm so sorry."

"I'll be fine. Let's just get the hell out of here."

∼

Thomas watched the blue Range Rover drive away with his heart. He'd done the right thing breaking up with her. He knew it was the right thing. She needed to be free, to finish her school, find a job, find another man.

He wanted to punch something when he thought of her with another man. But she was too smart, too young, too beautiful, and too rich to be with the likes of him. He was just a cowboy. Just a ranch hand. He had a pot full of money saved, because his needs were simple, and he made decent money working for the Kiplings.

But that didn't matter, he had to let her go. He knew she was mad at him. She hadn't looked at him since they'd walked out the door of her room. He couldn't blame her. Hell, he was mad at himself, and he's the one that did it. But he knew it was for the best.

He knew that the best thing in his life had just driven out of it. He'd never find another woman that he loved like he did her. He knew that for a fact. But because he loved her, he had to let her go. She deserved more than him. Eventually she would have resented him, seen him for what he was.

So, he'd let her go free. He didn't want her taking some crappy job just so she could stay near him. She needed to use her PhD, her intelligence, her strength. God it was going to kill him not to see her again.

She had a huge piece of his heart. It would never be whole again. She taken most of it with her. In some ways, he was glad she had it, he was glad he'd met her and loved her. Even if the pain, brought him to his knees.

He would go on working for the Kiplings and remember the beautiful woman who had been his, for three amazing weeks.

CHAPTER 23

The mine reclamation company was arriving today, on Valentine's Day of all days. Thomas couldn't care less, but Travis had asked him to take point with this team, too. Travis had explained that he wanted a couple of their own to be nearby, at least at the start. So, he and Lloyd were the most logical.

He didn't tell Travis that it would hurt his heart to be up at the mine with this new bunch of engineers. All the color had gone out of his life when Brenda had left a month ago and he didn't want to be anywhere near the place.

Some of the crew would stay at the big house, some had trailers of their own that they would park out by cabin two. Perhaps some of them would stay in cabin two. He didn't know how he would feel about that, so he chose not to think about it.

He heard vehicles pulling into the yard, so he went out to greet the arrivals. His feet faltered when a blue Range Rover Defender pulled to the side of the barn. It looked exactly like Brenda's. But it couldn't be, and he was stupid to think she was the only one that drove that model and color.

He got his feet moving again, until the woman herself got out of the car and stretched. Déjà vu smacked him upside the head, turning him to stone.

Lloyd whacked him on the back with one hand while he carried flowers in the other. "You really didn't keep in contact with the girls? Idiot."

Thomas shook his head. "No, I thought…"

Lloyd laughed. "I heard all about what you thought. Tracy and I had a good laugh about it. Well, come on we need to get the girls luggage to their rooms."

"Their rooms?"

"Yep, they are part of the reclamation company."

"But —"

"No buts, let's move. Travis is handling the others."

Thomas couldn't tear his eyes away from Brenda to verify. All he could do was move toward her, he hoped to hell he wasn't dreaming or hallucinating.

Brenda looked up, and said formally, "Hello Thomas, this is my luggage and that's Tracy's. I was told we'd be in the same rooms as before."

Thomas just nodded stupidly and grabbed her suitcases. She'd brought a lot more with her this time and he tried to think why that might be, but he couldn't get his brain to function. He followed in her wake. She was treating him like an acquaintance, and he didn't like it much.

When they got to her room, he carried the luggage in and set it where she directed. He heard the lock snick, and turned in time to catch the woman, as she launched herself into his arms and fastened her mouth to his, in a kiss so hot he was surprised the smoke detector didn't go off.

Finally, she let him breathe and slid down his body to sit on the bed. With a huge sigh she said, "That's better. I wanted to do that the minute I saw you, but didn't think my new boss would be amused."

"But you've got another semester of school."

"I'll finish up the last classes online. This company jumped at the chance to hire me and give Tracy an internship. She can do her thesis on the project. I'll add it to mine as a case study. But they hired me full time, with an impressive salary if I would join them and continue working on the project."

He wasn't sure how it all worked but he was thrilled to have her back again. He'd missed her like crazy.

"So, are you going to get over your stupid, 'I need to find my place' and let yourself be the place I want to be? Because I want you Thomas, not someone my age, or another engineer, or whatever other silly notion you have. I love you Thomas, you're my place."

He knelt in front of her and took her hands. "You're my place too, Brenda. I missed you like a limb. I love you. I don't know how to manage the future…"

She put her fingers over his mouth. "Perfect, we'll make plans for the future, later. We've got lots of time to decide on that, but the company I work for has plenty of opportunities over here on this side of the divide."

She looked at his mouth and her expression turned sly. "Do you think we have time before dinner to make love?"

He chuckled; it was only two. "I think we could manage it, but don't you need to check in with your boss or something?"

"No. I told them I would see them at dinner. Travis is taking them out to park their trailers out by cabin two. I told them I needed time to settle in. Unpack and stuff, but I would much rather get you naked. I can unpack any time."

He simply stood there grinning stupidly.

Brenda was glad to be back at the Rockin' K, it had been a long four weeks. A busy one, and she'd had to arrange for her classes to be online, then the career fair was the first of February and the mine reclamation company she'd signed up with had pushed hard to make that happen. Multiple interviews, a recruiting dinner, salary negotiations, the works. She wondered how much Steve had arranged, or if part of their desire for her had been because she was his grad student.

It didn't matter because she was thrilled to be back with Thomas and the mine reclamation was going to be a fun project to work on. She'd be working with top notch experts in the field and had already talked to the head engineer about what they'd found. The guy listened to her every word and had assured her she would be his right-hand woman.

After that, she'd decided, on the spot, to take their offer. What she needed to finish for school was minor. A couple of final classes and the presentation of her thesis. She'd have to go back to present her thesis but that was easy enough to do, it was only a two-hour drive. The plan was to go down the night before and grab a hotel room where she could practice away from everyone.

She was very happy with her life and she knew she and Thomas would figure out the future.

EPILOGUE

Thomas sat in the audience, waiting for the commencement to begin. He was sitting between Brenda's parents. Her mother and boyfriend on one side, and her father and his girlfriend on the other. It was awkward.

On the drive out of the mountains, Brenda had talked about her surprise that they were attending at all.

"They didn't come to my undergrad graduation, why are they coming this time?"

Tracy said from the backseat. "I'm sure they regretted not coming the first time."

Brenda shook her head. "I doubt that. But I guess I'm glad they did come this time. Will you sit with them, Thomas?"

"If you want me to."

"Yes, please. That lets you and Lloyd off the hook," she said to Tracy.

Tracy grinned. "Excellent, I've sat through dinner with each of them once, and that was enough for me."

"I still can't believe they came at all."

But here they were, so he'd met them. They seemed nice

enough. They were polite, and they didn't roll their eyes or look down at the cowboy

The commencement speeches, and all the rigmarole took forever. But when Brenda walked across that stage, he was so damn proud of her. He let out a whoop. She knew it was him and waved, her smile was huge.

After graduation she came towards him across the grass, he pulled her up and swung her around, then whispered in her ear, "I'm so damn proud of you, so damn proud." There were tears in her eyes when he set her down.

Her mother gave her a light hug and air kissed both her cheeks; the boyfriend gave her a much more enthusiastic hug which made Thomas twitch.

Her father gave her a hug and kissed her on the forehead. "Good job, Brenda, good job." The arm candy merely smiled.

Thomas asked, "Do you folks have time to go out to lunch with us?"

Her mother took her boyfriend's arm. "Oh no, we need to get back to the airport."

"We've got plans for this afternoon," her father said with a sly grin toward the arm candy.

He could tell Brenda was disappointed, but he doubted that they noticed, they were much more interested in their own feelings, than hers.

Smiling she said, "Thanks for coming. Mom, Dad."

Her mom patted her arm. "Oh honey, we had the time."

"Well, I'm glad you got to meet Thomas."

"We are too," her father said, then looked at Thomas. "Take good care of our girl."

"I will, you can count on it."

Once her parents and their friends, had driven off, Thomas tried to steer Brenda away from concern about her parent's attitude. He said, "Where would you like to eat?"

He could see her shake off the melancholy and turn to him with a bright expression. "Let's go to my favorite Mexican place."

"Okay."

Brenda sent Tracy a text with the location for lunch.

They walked to the little hole in the wall restaurant. There was a huge line from all the other people going there after the graduation ceremonies, but they didn't mind, they had all day. They were given a little beeper kind of thing, so they could go sit outside, which they did, it was a bright, clear sunny day in Grandville. The skies so blue it almost hurt to look at them.

They sat out on one of the rock walls that lined the sidewalk.

Thomas was nervous. His hands were sweaty. But they had a beautiful day. And even though he'd planned to do this differently, he had the opportunity now, so he took it.

"Brenda?"

Her face was lifted toward the sun, her eyes closed. "Yes, Thomas."

"You know I love you."

A smile tilted her lips. "Yes, and I love you, too."

"Well, I was wondering if you would be interested in making it a permanent relationship with me."

She opened her lovely violet eyes and looked at him with one lifted eyebrow. "What did you have in mind?"

He pulled in a deep breath. "Brenda, will you marry me?"

"Marry you?"

"Yes. Marry me. I bought some land from the Kipling's. So, I can build us our own house. And when you have to travel, I'll wait for you. Or sometimes I can come with you. So, will you marry me? Maybe have a baby or two with me?" he was babbling, he forced himself to stop and let her answer.

Tears ran down her face. "Yes, Thomas. I will marry you and have a baby or two."

"Excellent."

"How soon do you think we can have the house built?"

"Well, they usually take six months or so, at least."

Perfect. We'll get married in six months or so and move in. I don't want a huge wedding, but I want some of the trappings.

"Whatever you want, darlin'." He pulled the ring out of his pocket, handed her the box.

She opened it. "Oh, Thomas. It's so beautiful."

It wasn't a huge diamond he knew that, but all around it were little rubies, in a circle. And a second circle of emeralds.

She looked up. "Christmas colors?"

"Yes. After all, it was Christmas when I fell in love with you. But if you want other stones—"

She put her hand over his mouth. "It's so romantic. I fell in love with you over Christmas, too. It's just right."

He took it out of the box and slid it onto her hand. It fit perfectly.

He laid his mouth on hers and they kissed for long minutes. They might have kept on kissing if not for the buzzer from the restaurant. It signaled that it was time to go in, their table was ready.

Tracy and Lloyd joined them at the door.

"Have you been crying? Did your parents—"

Brenda's smile could have lit the entire town, the entire front range. "Happy tears." She held out her hand. "Thomas asked me to marry him, and I said yes."

Tracy squealed and crushed her in a hug. "I'm so happy for you."

"I'm happy for me, too."

While Tracy exclaimed over the ring, Lloyd slapped Thomas on the back, then kissed Brenda's cheek.

The hostess cleared her throat and asked, "Would you like to be seated? It looks like champagne might be in order."

Thomas said, "It is indeed."

THE END

The Helluva Engineer series continues with Her Forever Man where Tracy and Lloyd work together on the mine contaminating the Rockin' K ranch.

If you enjoyed this story, please consider leaving a review at your favorite retailer, Bookbub, or Goodreads.
Thanks!

ALSO BY SHIRLEY PENICK

LAKE CHELAN SERIES
First Responders
The Rancher's Lady: A Lake Chelan novella
Hank and Ellen's story
Sawdust and Satin: Lake Chelan #1
Chris and Barbara's story
Designs on Her: Lake Chelan #2
Nolan and Kristen's story
Smokin': Lake Chelan #3
Jeremy and Amber's story
Fire on the Mountain: Lake Chelan #4
Trey and Mary Ann's story
The Fire Chief's Desire: Lake Chelan #5
Greg and Sandy's story
Mysterious Ways: Lake Chelan #6
Scott and Nicole's story
Conflict of Interest: Lake Chelan #7
David and Jacqueline's story
Another Chance for Love: Lake Chelan #8
Max and Carol's story
Frames: Lake Chelan #9
Terri and Deborah's story
Christmas in Lake Chelan: Lake Chelan #10

Ted and Tammy's story

The Author's Lady Librarian: Lake Chelan #11

Patty Anne and Gideon's story

The Fire Chief's Surprise: Lake Chelan #12

Greg and Sandy's short story

Hello Again: Lake Chelan #13

Janet and Everett's story

(Previously part of the Goodbye Doesn't Mean Forever anthology)

Three's a Crowd: Lake Chelan #14

Kyle and Samantha's story

(Previously part of the Valentine Kisses anthology)

BURLAP AND BARBED WIRE SERIES

Colorado Cowboys

A Cowboy for Alyssa: Burlap and Barbed Wire #1

Beau and Alyssa's story

Taming Adam: Burlap and Barbed Wire #2

Adam and Rachel's story

Tempting Chase: Burlap and Barbed Wire #3

Chase and Katie's story

Roping Cade: Burlap and Barbed Wire #4

Cade and Summer's story

Trusting Drew: Burlap and Barbed Wire #5

Drew and Lily's story

Emma's Rodeo Cowboy: Burlap and Barbed Wire #6

Emma and Zach's story

SADDLES AND SECRETS SERIES

Wyoming Wranglers

The Lawman: Saddles and Secrets #1

Maggie Ann and John's story

The Watcher: Saddles and Secrets #2

Christina and Rob's story

The Rescuer: Saddles and Secrets #3

Milly and Tim's story

The Vacation: Saddles and Secrets Short Story #4

Andrea and Carl Ray's story

(Previously Part of the Getting Wild in Deadwood anthology)

The Neighbor: Saddles and Secrets #5

Terri and Rafe's story

HELLUVA ENGINEER SERIES

Helluva Engineer: Helluva Engineer #1

Patricia and Steve's story

Christmas at the Rockin' K: Helluva Engineer #2

Brenda and Thomas's story

Her Forever Man: Helluva Engineer #3

Tracy and Lloyd's story

ABOUT THE AUTHOR

What does a geeky math nerd know about writing romance?

That's a darn good question. As a former techy I've done everything from computer programming to international trainer. Prior to college I had lots of different jobs and activities that were so diverse, I was an anomaly.

None of that qualifies me for writing novels. But I have some darn good stories to tell and a lot of imagination.

I have lived in Colorado, Hawaii and currently reside in Washington. Going from two states with 340 days of sun to a state with 340 days of clouds, I had to do something to perk me up. And that's when I started this new adventure called author. Joining the Romance Writers of America and two local chapters, helped me learn the craft quickly and was a ton of fun.

My family consists of two grown children, their spouses, two adorable grand-daughters, and one grand dog. My favorite activity is playing with my granddaughters!

When the girls can't play with their amazing grandmother, my interests are reading and writing, yay! I started reading at a young age with the Nancy Drew mysteries and have continued to be an avid reader my whole life. My favorite reading material is romance, but occasionally if other stories creep into my to-be-read pile, I don't kick them out.

Some of the strange jobs I have held are a carnation grower's worker, a trap club puller, a pizza hut waitress, a software engineer, an international trainer, and a business program manager. I took welding, drafting and upholstery in high school, a long time ago, when girls didn't take those classes, so I have an eclectic bunch of knowledge and experience.

And for something really unusual… I once had a raccoon as a pet.

Join with me as I tell my stories, weaving real tidbits from my life in with imaginary ones. You'll have to guess which is which. It will be a hoot!

Contact me:

www.shirleypenick.com
To sign up for Shirley's Monthly Newsletter, sign up on my website or send email to shirleypenick@outlook.com, subject newsletter.

Follow me:

Printed in Great Britain
by Amazon